Suddenly this great big, good-looking guy came up and peered into my face, grinning.

"Could I help you up the steps?" he asked.

I tried frantically to think of something to say, but my mind was blank.

"Maybe you didn't hear me." He grinned, crooking his arm genteelly through mine as he guided me up the steps. I noticed his eyes were sky blue, and his hair was dark brown with tints of auburn.

"Do you know what room the astronomy club meets in?" I asked.

"Sure do. I'm the president of the club."

Dear Readers,

We at Silhouette would like to thank all our readers for your many enthusiastic letters. In direct response to your encouragement, we are now publishing *three* FIRST LOVEs every month.

As always FIRST LOVEs are written especially for and about you—your hopes, your dreams, your ambitions.

Please continue to share your suggestions and comments with us; they play an important part in our pleasing you.

I invite you to write to us at the address below:

Nancy Jackson
Senior Editor
Silhouette Books
P.O. Box 769
New York, N.Y. 10019

MY LUCKY STAR
Becka Cassiday

First Love from Silhouette

Published by Silhouette Books New York

America's Publisher of Contemporary Romance

SILHOUETTE BOOKS, a Simon & Schuster Division of
GULF & WESTERN CORPORATION
1230 Avenue of the Americas, New York, N.Y. 10020

ISBN: 0-671-53340-1

First Silhouette Books printing February, 1983

10 9 8 7 6 5 4 3 2 1

For Jodi, my own cat-lover,
who is an ocean of inspiration

My dad sold everything when we moved into Grandfather Barclay's old house in Seattle. At least he sold everything that had belonged to him and Mom. I got to keep my stereo, records, and a few other things. The rest of our stuff was auctioned off in a big barn just south of Federal Way.

When we moved into this ancient, rambling two-story out near the zoo, Dad gave me the telescope kit I'd wanted for so long. It was beautiful, even though I knew it was a bribe to make me less miserable.

I set up a room in the attic where I could grind the six-inch mirror until it was concave-shaped to exacting specifications. It was a long process which involved countless steps of careful stroking with coarse-grained sand, graduating down to the finest powder.

I didn't care. The work would take my mind off moving to Seattle and help fill the lonely hours without Mom. Not that I needed much more to fill my hours. To help save money for my college education, which would start in two years, my dad had offered to pay me thirty dollars a week if I'd watch my little brother and sister all summer.

Today, the long vacation seemed to stretch before me like the endless expanse of the Pacific. I was glad it was Monday because tonight the local astronomy club would meet at the library. I would get a chance to meet a few kids who shared my interest in the stars. Maybe, if I were really lucky, some of those kids would go to my high school when the semester started next fall.

I spent all afternoon deciding what to wear to the meeting and finally settled on jeans, blue Cherokee wedges, and a flowered blouse that had lace all around the neck. The outfit wasn't too dressy in case this turned out to be a very casual club. And I liked the way my eyes looked when I wore this shirt, kind of a darker blue than usual.

I brushed my hair for twenty minutes before pulling the top back and catching it up in a rubber band at the back of my head. Beth, my nine-year-old sister, braided the hair in the rubber band and I brushed the rest down over my shoulders.

"That looks pretty," Beth said, running her small fingers through the light brown strands, messing up the whole effect.

I looked at her gorgeous blond hair, wondering for the millionth time why she had inherited all of Mom's beauty. Beth's hair was really wavy, not curly enough to be a problem, just long, blond, and wavy the way I'd always imagined Rapunzel's hair was in the fairy tale.

Rooster came into my room and leaned against the door watching us. He was only six and most of the time he was the biggest pest I'd ever seen. But sometimes, like just before bedtime, he would crawl up in my lap and lay his head on my shoulder and it made me want to hug him so hard it hurt. But I usually wouldn't. I guess I didn't want him to know that I missed Mom as much as he did.

Nobody knew that. Not even Dad. I'd covered those feelings up so much that sometimes even I couldn't find them. The night we moved into this dumb old house, I was so lonely I wanted to cry when I climbed into Grandpa's old bed in the front bedroom upstairs. But I couldn't. I'd simply decided I would never love anybody again like I had loved Mom.

So anyway, Rooster was leaning on the door watching Beth and me and he got this silly grin on his face. "The more you brush your hair, Staci, the more it's just exactly the color of corn flakes."

"Get out of here, Rooster," I shouted. He always said my hair was the same color as corn flakes and it really bugged me. I guess because I had to admit he was right. It looked sort of light brown with little blond patches from the sun, maybe more like sugar frosted flakes in the summer. In the winter . . . well, it was just the color of corn flakes. My hair, like my freckles, was not one of my better features.

I looked at Grandpa's old wind-up alarm clock beside my bed. Everything in this house belonged to my grandparents before it became ours. It was six-thirty and I knew I'd better hurry if I wanted to be on time for the seven o'clock meeting. I had to walk five or six blocks to get to the library.

"Okay, you guys," I said. "Get out of my room and stay out while I'm gone. Dad says you're not allowed to touch my records, so don't forget."

"Big grouch," Rooster grumbled, sticking his foot further inside the room just to see if he could make me yell at him.

"I'm not going to braid your hair anymore, Staci," Beth said, letting her face get that scrunched-up look she used when she wanted to make me feel really guilty.

"Come on," I soothed. "I just don't want you messing up my stuff. You can come back in here after I get home." I looked around the high-ceilinged room filled with furniture that didn't belong to me and I wondered why I was being so possessive. There wasn't much here that I even cared that much about.

I scooted them out the door ahead of me and started for the stairs. My father was sitting in his usual place in front of the television, watching the evening news. I waved to him from the doorway.

"I'm leaving for the meeting, Dad. See you later."

"Hold on a minute," he said, pulling himself up out of the chair. "What time do you think you'll be home?"

I sucked in my breath and tried not to let my impatience show. I was already going to be late. "I'm not sure," I shrugged. "I've never attended this club's meetings before. Maybe they let out early. Maybe late."

He gave me a sharp questioning look as if he was trying to decide if I was being impertinent. "Well, I don't want you walking home after dark. Why don't you call when you get finished?"

"Oh, Dad." I was bouncing up and down, anxious to leave but mortified at the thought of calling my father to come and pick me up at the library. "It'll be fine if I walk. I do it all the time."

He lowered his eyebrows and scowled. "Not after dark you don't, Staci. I said call when the meeting is over and I'll bring the kids and pick you up. Maybe we can stop for an ice cream or something."

I groaned. There was no point discussing it

any further. Once my father scowled and looked at me like that, he'd made up his mind and absolutely nothing would change it. "Fine, Dad," I muttered. "I'll call you from the library."

"Have a good time," he grinned. "I hope you meet a lot of young people who share your interests. Maybe you can find someone to help you with your telescope project."

"Maybe so," I said, backing away and trying to get to the door. I stumbled over something and went sprawling backward, arms flailing the air. I landed on my back. There was a high-pitched howl and suddenly Rooster and Beth were crying and running after a gray streak that had taken off down the hall.

Harvey!

Grandfather Barclay's cat, Harvey, had been lying on the floor. I began to worry that she might be hurt.

Harvey was a female cat, a very pregnant female, that my brother had named for Grandpa three years ago when we found her beside the street. She was only a kitten then and Rooster was only three. I think maybe Rooster gave her such a strange name because of his own.

Dad always hollered at Beth and me for calling our brother Rooster. "His name is Rodney," Dad would say. But Rooster was so funny with his bright red hair and the cowlick that stood up at the crown no matter how hard we tried to plaster it down. Eventually Dad gave up and sometimes he even called my brother Rooster. It was one of those silly nicknames you start using and it sticks to the person like glue.

Beth came sulking back into the living room with Harvey clutched in her arms. The cat was big, obese really, and she looked kind of ridiculous hanging limply out both sides of Beth's arms while her swollen belly hung down like a water-filled balloon. Beth sank to the floor and started stroking the large gray cat and crooning to her.

"Is she all right?" I asked, trying to look at my watch without everybody seeing me.

"Yes," Beth said. "No thanks to you, Staci. You almost squashed her."

Rooster scooted up next to Beth on the floor and gave me his fiercest glare. "Cat squasher," he sneered.

"I didn't mean to," I sighed. "You know I wouldn't hurt her on purpose."

"You might," Beth said. "You don't like Harvey or this house or anything else in our family. You might squash her just to get even."

"Dad!" I wailed. "I've got to go."

He was watching all three of us with that half-amused, half-bewildered look I seemed to see more and more often on his face. "I know, Staci," he sighed. "The cat's all right and we know you didn't do it on purpose. Run along to your meeting or you'll be late."

"I'm already late," I mumbled. "The meeting's starting right now."

"So be a few minutes late," he said. "You've been waiting all week for this. Now get a move on."

I waved good-bye to Rooster and Beth who managed a perfect snarl-duet from their place on the floor with the cat. Harvey had kind of a baleful look on her face and I felt she was enjoying every minute of the attention.

Stupid cat.

I hurried out the front door, relieved to be away from my family for a little while and away from this awful house that wasn't even ours. The air was delightfully cool with a breeze blowing in off Puget Sound like it always did in the evenings. All around me were tall pine trees and everything smelled wonderfully fresh and clean.

My steps slowed as I got closer to the library. I hated the left-out feeling of being the "new kid." Maybe I could skip the meeting and just walk around the free-rolling hills.

No. I'd told my father I was going to the library and I'd better go. I never lied to him about things like this. Besides, if I didn't meet some people my own age pretty soon, I'd spend the whole summer feeling sorry for myself.

I could see the library up ahead now and my palms broke out with little beads of nervous perspiration. What if I pulled one of my usual stupid tricks like forgetting how to talk when I walked into the room? Lots of times, when I lie in bed imagining how things will be on the first day at my new high school, I imagine myself smiling confidently and saying marvelously clever things that will make all the kids want to be around me because I'm such a terrific human being.

But in reality, I usually stutter and stammer when I meet new people and if I say anything at all, it's usually something so dumb it would sound better coming out of Rooster or even Harvey.

I was standing at the bottom of the library steps now and my sweaty palms had given way to true panic. How many people would be here? Would they think I was a real weirdo?

Twice I started up the steps only to turn around and slink back to the bottom. All I knew about this meeting was that it was an astronomy club for young people and my dad had read about it on the bulletin board at the Safeway. Suddenly I didn't have much interest in going to the meeting. I could make the telescope on my own and learn everything else I needed to know from books.

While I was standing there trying to figure out some good excuse for going back home, this great big, good-looking guy came up and peered into my face, grinning.

"Could I help you up the steps?" he asked. "You seem to be having a little problem getting to the top."

I felt my cheeks burn and I knew my face

was red and flushed like it always got when I was embarrassed. I tried frantically to think of something clever to say but my mind was blank. We just stood there staring into each other's eyes.

"Maybe you didn't hear me," he grinned, crooking his arm genteelly like I was supposed to take hold of it and be guided up those stairs like an old lady. "If you need help going into the library, I'll be happy to assist."

"I was just doing an exercise," I stammered. "I am perfectly capable of climbing a flight of stairs."

He grinned again and I noticed his eyes were sky blue or maybe ocean blue. They looked exactly like the color you see in those little mountain lakes when the day is perfectly clear and the water seems to give back a reflection of the sky that is even bluer than the expanse above you. His hair was dark brown but it had beautiful tints of auburn in it and I had to look away for a minute to keep from sighing.

All in all, he was the most handsome guy I had ever seen and I couldn't think of anything to say. He offered his arm again and I took it, like a robot who's been wound up by a mad scientist. I felt like a fool but it was easier to follow this gorgeous guy quietly up the stairs than it was to trust myself to speak.

When we got to the top, he opened the big glass door with a flourish and bowed. "After you," he said.

I walked inside and then stopped, not having any idea where the meeting room was. I guess he couldn't see me through the dark glass because when he walked in, he crashed right into me. He didn't seem too amused and he stared at me for a minute before shaking my shoulders gently. "Are you okay there?" he asked, peering deeply into my eyes.

"Yes," I snapped, more embarrassed by my own bizarre behavior than angry at him. "I'm just new here and I don't know where to go for the astronomy meeting."

His eyes got really wide. "You're going to that?"

"Yes," I said. "What's wrong with that?"

He grinned again. "Nothing. I just figured anybody who had this much trouble navigating on earth wouldn't have enough courage to tackle the heavens."

"I manage all right," I said. "I'm even making my own telescope."

"How about that?" he smiled. "You should never judge a book by its cover or a girl by her stumbling."

I started to get really annoyed with him but he was laughing and I knew he was only kidding.

"Do you know what room the meeting is in?" I asked, trying to be a good sport.

"Sure do. I'm the president of the club." He smiled. "My name's B.J. Keller." He had hold of my arm again and was leading me toward some double doors that led off the right side of the lobby. "I'm late tonight because I had to take my mom to another meeting. Her car's in the shop. Everybody else should be here by now."

We were walking down a long hall and I could smell the pungent aroma of old books and frequently waxed floors. I had to look straight ahead to keep from staring at B.J. He was so gorgeous, such an absolute dream.

When we came to a door at the end of the hall he stopped, letting me enter the room ahead of him. I saw three or four telescopes at the front of the room. Boys, most of them about my age, were standing around in small groups visiting. A couple of guys were looking at some charts of constellations which were hanging from the ceiling. Everybody looked up expectantly when we entered the room.

"Sorry I'm late," B.J. said. "I found a damsel in distress on the front steps and it turned out she was looking for us."

"She is in distress then," one of the boys said. "Anybody who can't find something more exciting to do than come to this meeting has got to be in big trouble."

Everybody laughed.

Everybody except B.J. "I disagree." He glared.

The snickering stopped. "None of us are forced to be here," B.J. continued. "We love what we're doing and I think it's dumb when we go around apologizing just because there are a few kids who think we're space freaks and brains."

I agreed with him but I couldn't make my tongue maneuver well enough to tell him so. The others nodded, a few of them obviously embarrassed by having made fun of themselves.

"Okay," B.J. said. "Everybody find a seat." He looked at me. "What's your name?"

I held my breath, praying that my voice wouldn't fail me right now. "Staci," I mumbled. "Staci Callahan."

"Well, Staci"—he grinned—"you can mingle with these neanderthals in a minute and get acquainted. Most of our group is here." He looked around the room. "Where's Marlo?" he asked.

"She said she'd be late," someone answered.

"Well, I hope she gets here." He looked at me. "Marlo Cate is the only other girl in our group. I'm sure you'll be glad when she gets here."

I just nodded, wondering if I looked as dumb as I felt. I couldn't think of anything to say.

"Staci told me she's grinding her own telescope," B.J. announced. "I know a lot of you guys have wanted to start a project like that. If you're really interested you ought to talk to her and see if you can get some hints."

"No, no," I stammered. "I just got the kit

and I haven't even started yet. I'm sure I wouldn't be able to help anyone else."

Several of the guys were moving closer, apparently more interested in me as an amateur astronomer than they had initially been. We were discussing the merits of refracting versus reflecting telescopes when the door opened and a beautiful girl walked in. I tried not to stare at her but she was one of those girls you just naturally stare at.

Her hair was jet black and skimmed straight back off her face in a sleek, sophisticated French knot. There were fine wisps of hair around her forehead and cheeks and the overall impression was breathtaking. Her clothes were incredible. Designer jeans topped with an expensive white eyelet blouse with a standup collar that somehow made her look like Snow White in the movie I saw when I was a kid. Any second I expected her to break out singing, "I'm Wishing, I'm Wishing."

Her eyes were as black as her hair and she had liner and mascara flawlessly applied to both the top and bottom lashes. Suddenly I felt like a geranium that nobody had watered for five or six weeks. She gazed at me with dark eyes that were delicately shadowed in three shades of mauve. I wanted to crawl in a hole and hide but it was too late.

B.J. was striding forward like some thunderstruck kid looking at a brand-new bike he'd wanted for a hundred years. His face had this idiot expression on it and I could see he was going to introduce the two "girls" and make a big production out of it. Since there was no escape, I just stood there waiting for a drum roll or something.

"Marlo," B.J. gushed. "I'm glad you made it." He reached out and for one ghastly minute, I thought he was going to kiss her hand. Instead he grabbed hold of it and pulled her closer to me for the big introduction. "I want you to meet somebody," he said. His eyes had gone all squinty and soft.

"This is a new addition to our club," he said, smiling foolishly. "Her name is Staci Callahan and she's building her own telescope."

Marlo's eyes just barely moved as she studied me, from Cherokee wedges to stupid, pulled back baby hair that I was painfully conscious was the color of corn flakes. I wanted to back out of the room so Marlo would never see the little braid Beth had put in, the one I had thought was so cute only an hour ago.

Then Marlo smiled. If you could call it that. The corners of her mouth did move upward a tiny bit. But so did her nose. She looked as if she'd just been presented to an inferior Martian specimen. "I'm pleased to meet you," she said stiffly.

I stammered, looked down at my feet, and then tried to smile at Marlo with more warmth than I felt. "It's nice to meet you too."

The black, perfectly made-up eyes appraised me carefully, as if offended by the sight of my freckled nose and my lack of cosmetics. "You're making your own telescope?" she inquired.

"I'm trying," I stammered. "I just got the kit and I haven't started yet."

"My father bought me one of the largest models available. We keep it out by the pool. I just love to observe Saturn after a nice refreshing dip." She turned to B.J. "Are you still coming over this evening? Remember, Mars is supposed to be unusually close for viewing tonight."

He grinned and turned toward the rest of us. "What do you think? Shall we all go over to Marlo's and have a real treat? I guess you all know by now that Marlo's got one terrific new telescope."

Marlo just gazed at him with those coal-black eyes. "I'm sorry, B.J.," she purred. "But I didn't get permission from Daddy for anyone except you to come over." She blushed. "I don't know what I could have been thinking," she sighed. "Next time, of course, I'll arrange for the whole group to come."

B.J. seemed a little embarrassed. He shuffled his feet back and forth a couple times and then waved his arms over his head. "Okay. No big deal," he said. "We'll do it another time. Everybody take your seats and we'll get this meeting started. We're already running late."

I sat down next to a boy who introduced himself as Doug Wilson. The boy next to him was Stan Franke. I watched Marlo whisper something to B.J. before she took a seat in the front row right next to B.J. and the charts of the constellations. For some reason, I knew I was going to dislike Marlo Cate more than anybody I had ever met in my life. As the meeting progressed with a lengthy discussion about the newest scientific findings and pictures of the rings around Saturn, I longed with all my heart to be back in Federal Way with the kids I'd gone to school with all my life and the only house I'd ever lived in until two weeks ago.

B.J. called Doug to the front of the room and he gave a report on a week-long study he'd done observing Mars. Another one of the boys used the constellation charts and gave a short talk on how to locate any of the major stars.

Most of the time I watched B.J. He was still just as cute as he'd been when we met on the steps and that made me dislike Marlo all the more for monopolizing his time and attention. I was twisting the little braid at the back of my head nervously, wondering how I could even think about a guy like B.J. when he so obviously adored Marlo.

"Did you hear me, Staci?" Doug said.

My head jerked up and I stared at him in embarrassment. "I'm sorry," I said. "What did you say, Doug?"

He grinned and let his gaze fall on B.J. for a second as if letting me know he knew where my attention had been. "I asked you what size your telescope is."

"It's a six-inch reflecting. Or it will be when I finally get the grinding done."

"That's great. I made one last year." He smiled. "It's a big challenge and lots of work but I sure thought it was worth it. If you have any questions or need any help, just give me a call."

"Thanks," I said.

The meeting was ending. B.J. was reminding everyone to be sure to arrive on time next Monday since we were all going out to Mercer Island to observe Venus. Four members had large telescopes and they were taking all of them out there early.

"We're glad you came tonight, Staci," B.J. said. "Can we count on you next week?"

I just nodded and shuffled my feet nervously. One of my rubber soles caught on the waxed floor and made a loud embarrassing sound and I scrunched quickly down in my chair, feeling my face flame. Doug grinned and Marlo looked at me as if I were an alien reptile.

. Everybody was standing up and I tried to rise quickly so I could get out of the room fast. I didn't want any of these kids to hear me calling my dad to come and get me. Especially Marlo.

But B.J. grabbed my arm as I slunk past

him and I was trapped. "Wait up, Staci," he
said. "We can all walk out together."

"That's all right," I stammered. "I need to
be getting home."

"Have you got a car?" he asked.

Now I was really trapped. Marlo was gazing
at me with those coal-black eyes and I would
have sworn she was laughing behind that
immovable mask she wore for a face. I started
to shuffle my feet again, remembered the
awful sound my shoe had made before and
stood perfectly still. B.J. was looking at me.

"No," I finally said. "I don't drive yet. I
can't get my license until the end of next
semester."

"You're not sixteen?" Marlo asked incredu-
lously.

"Yes," I snapped. "I just wasn't sixteen soon
enough to take driver's ed last year."

"Do you need a ride?" B.J. asked patiently.

"No." I was getting more humiliated by the
second. "I live really close. I can walk." I tried
one more time to slip out of B.J.'s grasp so I
could get to the phone without anyone seeing
me.

"Nonsense," B.J. said. "I'll be glad to give
you a lift on my way over to Marlo's."

There was no way out of the situation now.
My father would be furious if I accepted a ride
with someone he hadn't met.

"I can't," I stammered, feeling warmth in
my cheeks again. "My dad told me to call him
after the meeting." I gave up all pretense,

shrugged my shoulders, and told the truth. "He'll be mad if I don't call him to come and get me."

Marlo was grinning maliciously now, victory written all over her finely formed features. "That's all right, B.J.," she purred. "The little girl won't need a ride. Her dad and mom are picking her up."

Suddenly I was out of the room and halfway down the hall without knowing for sure how I'd gotten there. I didn't dislike Marlo Cate anymore. I hated her! How dare she make fun of my mother? She was one of the meanest girls I'd ever met.

The librarian pretended not to notice my tears when I asked her if I could use the phone. Dad said it would be a few minutes before he got there so when I hung up, I hurried back to the historical section and lost myself in the rows of thick musty books so no one would find me if they came looking.

Ten minutes later I walked cautiously out to the lobby and, not seeing anyone from the astronomy club, I hurried outside where I saw our station wagon. Rooster and Beth were hanging out the back windows holding huge double-dip ice cream cones.

"We got you a fudge-ripple!" Rooster screamed. I ducked my head, trying to look around carefully to make sure everyone was gone. Marlo was standing beside a red Trans-Am watching my every move. B.J. was grinning at me and he waved cheerfully.

I felt my entire body slump as I climbed into the front seat and accepted the dripping ice cream cone Rooster thrust into my hand. "Thanks, Dad," I said. "Thanks a lot."

He grinned at me. "Anytime, honey. We didn't mind coming for you at all. Did we, kids?"

The next day I got up early to fix breakfast for my dad and start the laundry before Rooster and Beth got up. I wanted to have most of the day to work on my telescope. I filled a paper sack with the kids' favorite toys so I could take them into the attic with me. I was hoping they would think of the whole thing as kind of an adventure or something and not fight and cause a lot of problems.

Dad kissed me on the cheek before he left for work. Watching him, I thought how he seemed happier in this house than he had in our old place in Federal Way. I felt guilty for wanting to go back so badly. Maybe here, at last, Dad would begin to live again, forget his grief about Mom. Something about the bounce in my father's step made me wish there was a place where both of us could heal quickly and get on with the business of living.

After Dad left, I set cereal bowls and fruit juice out for Beth and Rooster. Usually they slept until at least eight. If they slept that late today, I'd have time to finish the laundry, make my bed and Dad's, and vacuum the den. That would leave almost all day to work on my telescope. When I thought about starting the delicate grinding process, I got butterflies in my stomach.

The kit had been expensive and I knew I wouldn't be able to replace it if I messed up. The instructions were quite clear, however, and it would be hard to do any harm in the first few steps. After that, I might have to take Doug up on his offer to help. One thing I knew, if it took the rest of my life I would make that telescope and show B.J. that some girls didn't have to have their fathers buy them expensive, custom-made equipment.

Just as I got the vacuum cleaner out and uncoiled the cord, Rooster wandered into the den with Beth right behind him.

"I'm hungry, Staci," he whined. "I don't want cereal either. Fix me some bacon and eggs."

"I want pancakes," Beth said.

They were in bad moods, picking and swatting at each other behind my back. I saw Beth swing her foot out and kick Rooster. That was all it took. They were off, running through the house, screaming, kicking, and tumbling.

This was going to be a horrible day unless I found some way to settle them down.

"All right," I yelled, trying to intercept them as they raced through the room again. "I'll fix anything you want for breakfast if you'll quit fighting. We're going to have a nice time in the attic after breakfast. You can play with all your toys while I work on my telescope."

"Not me," Beth said. "It's hot in that dumb old attic."

"Me either," Rooster said. "I think there's a monster up there."

"Come on, you guys," I said, trying not to lose my temper. "There's no monster in the attic and it's not at all hot with the window open. You can see Lake Washington and Mount Ranier from there and you'll like it. I promise."

We all walked to the kitchen where I fixed bacon and eggs for Rooster and pancakes for Beth. It took more than an hour to feed them and get the dishes done. After that, I went back and vacuumed the den before pulling out the sack of toys I'd prepared for the kids.

"Now," I announced. "It's time to go upstairs. You can both help with the telescope once in a while if you're real good." I held out the sack. "Here's all your favorite stuff, so let's go."

In unison, as if they'd planned it, Rooster and Beth sat down and stared at me without moving.

Harvey waddled past and Rooster grabbed

her, holding onto her thick middle and glaring at me with unrelenting eyes. Beth reached over and stroked the cat.

"Have you fed Harvey?" Beth asked.

I flinched with guilt because I had forgotten to feed her that morning. It was the second time this week that I'd let that happen. I shook my head, waiting for the kids' biting accusations.

But they didn't say a word, just stood up together and carried that fat, bulging cat to the kitchen where I could hear them opening cupboard doors and slamming things around as they prepared a meal that was probably better than the one I'd fixed for them. I winced at the thought of the mess they were making and mentally subtracted another hour from the time I'd have to work up in the attic.

I walked into the kitchen and found them both on the floor, kneeling beside Harvey and feeding her left-over eggs, cat food, and a piece of bacon. The kitchen, just as I'd feared, was a total disaster.

"That wasn't very thoughtful, you guys," I snapped. "Now I have to clean this mess up again."

"We don't care," Rooster said. "You were trying to kill Harvey by not feeding her. You didn't think we'd notice her starving 'cause she's so fat." His face was all scrunched up and he looked as though he were going to cry.

"That's not true, Rooster, I forgot to feed her

and I'm really sorry. I wouldn't want anything to happen to Harvey any more than you would."

"Ha!" Beth sat like a robot, stroking the cat's fat gray body automatically, not lifting her eyes to meet mine.

"Come on," I begged. "You know I didn't forget on purpose."

"You tried to squash her yesterday," Rooster said, as if that was all the evidence needed to implicate me as a known cat killer for the rest of my life.

"It was an accident," I yelled. "You guys think more of that cat than you do of . . ." I stopped myself, refrained from saying the words that had been on the tip of my tongue.

Beth was standing up, staring at me with tears in her eyes. "You were going to starve Harvey!" She was really crying now. Huge teardrops were rolling down her cheeks.

I watched my pretty little sister, who looked so much like my mother, run out of the room. Rooster got up without a word and followed Beth. I slumped down on the floor next to Harvey and stretched my legs out, barely noticing that my tennis shoes were in a puddle of milk.

Why couldn't I be more like the kids? Why couldn't I just go ahead and love something the way they loved this cat? But I already knew the answer. Love wasn't safe. Love hurt because sometimes the person or thing you loved disappeared from your life without even giving you a chance to say good-bye.

I buried my face in the soft gray fur of Harvey's coat. For a few minutes I stroked her fur and felt comforted for the first time since Mom died two years ago. Then I went to find the kids. They were in Beth's room. They were sitting on the floor looking at some of Grandfather Barclay's old photo albums. They looked up at me when I entered the room but neither one of them spoke. I sat down beside them and slowly we turned the pages, looking at pictures of our grandparents as a young couple and then seeing photos of Aunt Sally as a baby and finally Mom.

One of the pictures showed Mom eating a birthday cake with eight candles. I drew in my breath involuntarily. The picture could have been Beth.

"How come there's a picture of you in Grandpa's book?" Rooster asked, turning to Beth and looking at her strangely.

"That's Mother," I said, turning the page quickly.

Some of the photos were of Grandpa and Grandma after they were older. Not old like they finally got, but older. Rooster leaned way down close to the book and studied the pictures.

"How come Grandpa died?" he asked, looking at me at last.

"Because he was old, Rooster. He was eighty-nine."

"How old was Mom?"

There it was. A question I either couldn't or didn't want to answer.

"How old was Mom?" Rooster repeated.

"She was thirty-four, Rooster," I mumbled.

"Is that old?"

"No, Rooster. It's not old. Mother got sick when she was young. It's not supposed to happen that way."

"But, Staci," Beth said. I looked at her reluctantly but just as I did the doorbell rang and I leaped up off the floor to run and answer it.

I reached the door and pulled it open. B.J. Keller was standing on the porch and I nearly fainted. "H-hello," I stammered. "How in the world did you ever find my house?"

He grinned. "I'm a private detective. It's my secondary hobby," he laughed.

I knew I was staring and I had to force myself to remember routine formalities. "Won't you come in?"

"I can only stay a few minutes. I just wondered how you were coming on your telescope," he said, stepping inside and glancing around the house. I was glad that I'd taken the time to go back and vacuum.

"Really," I finally said. "How did you find my house?"

"I asked my sister who works down at the Safeway if she knew who you were and she said you and your dad came in all the time. She was pretty sure you lived on Washington

Drive so I just asked a few neighbors until I found one who could tell me which was your house."

"You really are a detective," I said. "But I'm afraid you've wasted your trip. I haven't had a chance to start working on my telescope."

He looked at me under lowered brows. "How long have you had that kit, Staci?"

"Two weeks," I said.

"Are you really serious about astronomy?"

"Of course I am. It's just that I'm watching my little brother and sister today and I haven't had a chance to do anything else."

He looked so large, formidable, and disapproving as he stood there in our house. I doubted if he ever had to babysit all day every day. He wouldn't understand even if he knew the circumstances.

Still, I couldn't help but be attracted to him with those broad shoulders and that gorgeous dark hair. I thought I caught a whiff of aftershave lotion and I wondered if he had to shave very often.

"Most girls aren't serious about things like astronomy," he said. "In fact, I've never met a girl who took any of the sciences seriously. I was hoping you were different."

"I am serious," I said, hearing my voice rise a little and feeling a flush of anger in my cheeks. "I told you I had to watch my little brother and sister today."

"Do you watch them every day?"

"As a matter of fact," I snapped, "I do."

"Look, it's really none of my business," B.J. said. "I told you I was just hoping you were different. Besides, I actually came over here to apologize for the rotten way Marlo acted last night. She's a nice person but sometimes she isn't very sensitive to other people."

"No problem," I said. "I'm sure Marlo and I will work our differences out in our own way. Do you want a Coke or something?"

He glanced around. "If it's all right. I mean if it won't interfere with your babysitting."

"It's fine," I said, relieved that he would stay a little while.

B.J. sat down in the living room and I hurried to the kitchen to get us each a Coke. When I returned, both of the kids were in the room with him, asking about a hundred stupid questions a minute.

I handed B.J. his Coke and turned to Rooster and Beth. "Why don't both of you go on and play for a while?" I asked.

"We want to stay here," Beth said, flopping heavily onto the couch beside B.J. and bouncing a slosh of Coke out of his glass.

Rooster stood watching B.J. dab at the drops. "Are you Staci's boyfriend?" he asked. I wanted to die right then but I should have known Rooster wasn't through. "She had a different boyfriend in Federal Way. His name was Dave and he never did anything except look at dumb old stars. I hope you don't look at stars all the time."

B.J. smiled at Rooster. "As a matter of fact," he said, "I do."

This didn't faze Rooster a bit. "The only guy I like," he went on conversationally, "is Andy next door. He never looks through telescopes. Andy likes electric race sets. But Staci doesn't like Andy. She says he's boring."

I looked at B.J., hoping I could somehow apologize with my eyes, but he didn't return my glance. He was still wiping at the Coke stain on his pants.

"Would you like to see my telescope kit?" I asked, trying to break the tension in the room.

B.J. stood up. "Sure. Why not?" He allowed a wide berth as he went around Rooster and Beth and crossed the room.

He followed me up the steep stairs to the attic and I showed him the table and the work area I'd set up. It was close to the window so I'd have plenty of light.

"This is a good kit, Staci," B.J. said. I could tell by the look in his eyes that he wasn't kidding.

"Thank you. I waited quite a while to get it."

He was even more enthusiastic as we went over the instructions and he looked at the little jars of sand and powder. "I remember when I first started mine," B.J. said. "It seemed like an impossible task when I looked at all the stuff. But I worked on it some every day and pretty soon it was ready to send off for the mirror surface."

"I don't even know where to send it when I'm ready," I said.

"Oh, I'll give you the address. Who's going to help you check the reflection?"

I shrugged my shoulders. "I sort of know how it's done but I'm sure I can't do it alone."

B.J. grinned. "Well, as pretty as you are, Staci, there will probably be ten guys fighting over the chance to help."

My breath caught in my throat and I found myself staring at my feet again. B.J. had said I was pretty! I knew his words would make this whole rotten day better than I had thought it could ever be.

I really liked B.J. and I wished I were beautiful and witty. I also wished Marlo Cate would move to Florida or someplace even further away. As long as she was around, B.J. would never really notice me.

We started back down the stairs and I was feeling good about B.J., the telescope and even my long summer with the kids. Just as we reached the bottom of the attic steps and B.J. pushed the door open, I heard a terrible crash, a splash, and a yowl of rage.

I looked at B.J. and he was absolutely drenched. Rooster was staring at me with a look of total terror. I could see Beth in the hall, holding her sides, doubled over with laughter. I knew what had happened. Rooster had planned one of his treacherous tricks. With Beth's help, he'd placed a pail of water on top of the door, thinking I would get drenched when we came downstairs. Instead, it had been B.J. I had never seen poor Rooster so scared and, mad as I was, I felt sorry for him.

B.J. turned toward me, his face distorted with rage. "I don't know where your parents go all the time, Staci. I don't know why they leave these kids with you, but I do know this is the most obnoxious kid I have ever met." With that, B.J. hurried toward the stairs.

"I'm sorry," I stammered. "I know it was a terrible trick but he meant it for me, B.J. He didn't know you'd open the door."

"I don't care, Staci. I've got to see Marlo in a few minutes and now I'll have to go home and change." He stalked down to the lower landing and turned to face me again. "I'm not coming back to visit *you* again, Staci. This place is dangerous!"

I heard the front door slam before I could reach the bottom of the stairs. I leaned my forehead against the wall and cried softly. Maybe after two years of not letting myself cry, I was going to get it all out in one day.

Rooster came up behind me and patted my arm softly. And suddenly I was furious with B.J. for the things he had said about my parents leaving the raising of Rooster and Beth in my hands.

In Federal Way it had been easy. All my friends knew me and they knew what had happened in our family. Here, it looked like I was going to have to endure one remark after another about my mother unless I explained to everybody that she had died. That, I decided, I wouldn't do.

I stooped down and gathered Rooster into my arms. "It's all right," I whispered. "I know you didn't mean to hit him with the pail of water. It wouldn't be necessary, Rooster, B.J.'s all wet anyway. But no more tricks when my friends are here!"

Together, the three of us went to the kitchen where I fixed lunch. Harvey was curled up on the floor near the stove and I looked at her enormous bulging sides, wondering how long before the kittens would be born. There was something about the idea of Harvey becoming a mother that scared me a little. I didn't want to get too close to the situation, get to loving that silly cat and her babies and then have something happen to one of them.

I looked at the clock while I cleaned up the kitchen after lunch. It was two-fifteen and I hadn't even started on the telescope. Dad would be in at five-thirty. Dinner needed to be on the stove by five. I'd be lucky if I managed to work on the telescope an hour a day. I was crying when I felt Rooster and Beth throw their arms around my waist and hug me while I worked.

Then they started crying too. I kneeled on the floor, holding both of the kids tight. Harvey moved in and out between our legs and knees, rubbing her soft head against all three of us and purring loudly.

I wished for the millionth time that Mom was here to make everything all right once again.

3

Thursday morning I was finally working on my telescope with Rooster and Beth playing happily beside me. I had barely begun the first step, stroking slowly back and forth on the pristine glass surface with a coarse-grained sand, when I heard the doorbell ring. I wiped my hands and hurried downstairs with Rooster and Beth right on my heels.

When I peered out the peep-hole, I groaned. It was Andy Warren, the boy next door. He was carrying a big dish of something and I knew his mother must have sent over another meal. She kept doing that and it made me feel funny. I always returned the bowl, thanked her for being so thoughtful, and Mrs. Warren would always give me a big hug and tell me how she'd like to help more if I'd only let her.

Andy banged on the door with his fist and reluctantly I let him in. "Hi ya. What's up, Andy?" I stumbled a little as Rooster jumped up and down like a ball beside me. Rooster absolutely adored Andy and was always excited and wild when he came over.

Andy smiled a gigantic smile that used to contain more silver than the train tracks around Union Station. But he'd had his braces removed last year. "Oh, you know my mother. She thinks your whole family will starve if she doesn't take every precaution. She made two meatloafs early this morning, one for us and one for you. She said you should set this in the refrigerator and put it in the oven about four." He handed me the bowl and then walked over to the couch and flopped down. Rooster was right behind him and he sat down, too.

I hurried to the kitchen to put the meatloaf away, wondering how long Andy intended to stay. I sure didn't want to give up my first day of work just to sit around talking. Andy was the only person I knew who I was sure would be going to high school with me next fall. He was a year older than me but we would be in the same grade because Andy had been held back in the first grade since he'd contracted every childhood illness in one year.

I wandered back to the living room. "I have a lot of work to do this morning, Andy. Do you think you could come back later?"

"What do you have to do?" he asked.

"Maybe I could help. If I go home my mom will just come up with thirty chores that absolutely have to be done today."

"I'm working on my telescope," I said. "It's the first chance I've had all week to do it. I don't know how all this housework takes so much time, but it does. It seems like I have to get up at five A.M. if I even hope to do something for myself."

"You sound just like my mother." He grinned. "I'll tell you what, Staci. I'll go upstairs and watch the kids while you work. Maybe we can talk a little and it will make the job more fun."

I thought about all the work I'd accomplished before he arrived but decided not to say anything. I'd known Andy since we both were toddlers and my family spent holidays and weekends here at Grandpa's. Friends like that couldn't be put off *all* the time.

"Fine, Andy," I finally said. "Come on upstairs. Maybe you can help the kids catch the dragon."

I hurried up ahead of them but not fast enough to avoid hearing Rooster explain the whole dragon game. Andy was laughing and going along with the story so well that I could tell Rooster and Beth were becoming more and more certain there might actually be a dragon hiding in the attic.

While I started back to work, Andy sat down on the floor very close to my table and watched me. "You really enjoy all that stuff with telescopes and stars, don't you, Staci?" he said.

I nodded, trying to concentrate on my work. "What are you planning to do when you grow up?"

I looked at him, wondering if I should tell the truth. My plans for the future were pretty private to me and I rarely discussed them. But there was something about Andy Warren that always seemed to get me talking. It had been that way for years. Even when I was little and would visit my grandparents, my mother would say, "Go on out and play with Andy, Staci. He loves to have you around so much," I would go grumbling out the door but I'd always end up having a great time and gripe like crazy when I was called in for supper.

So I looked at Andy and decided to tell him what I wanted to be. "I'm going to be an astronaut," I said, waiting for him to start laughing like a fool and carrying on.

"I think that's great," Andy said. "I'm already seventeen and I can't seem to make up my mind what I want to do. Nothing seems to grab me." His head was bent forward and his shoulders were slumped. I could tell he was really down and needed to talk.

"So. What's the big deal?" I said lightly. "Lots of kids don't even decide on a major until their second or third year of college."

"I'm too old to keep playing at life like I've got another ten years before college. In just two years we'll be off to school, and four years after that we'll be expected to enter the business world or whatever."

"Not me," I muttered. "After college I'll have to wait for ages just to see if I get accepted into the astronaut program. Once I pass that hurdle, I'll still have years of training." I smiled, feeling the excitement of my life-long dream bubble within me. "I don't care though, Andy. It's the only thing I've ever wanted to do. The thought of actually traveling into space gets me so excited I can hardly stand it."

"I told you you were lucky," Andy said. "I don't even have a hobby that turns me on like you with your telescope. I'm still like some kid who likes to throw a football around with Rooster and spend my weekends down on the beach." He sighed and turned to watch Rooster and Beth crawl under and over the beams and rafters at the dark end of the attic in search of the elusive dragon. "I mean," he finally added, "I really enjoy playing like that. I have fun with my life and dread growing up. It doesn't seem to bother you at all."

"But it does, Andy. I'm scared that I might never get accepted into the space program. I'm scared that I'll let my family down in some way if I fail. I'm scared to let myself love . . ." I stopped, surprised at the intimate things I was about to reveal. "I'm scared of lots of things, Andy," I finally said. "Just like you."

He was watching me now, instead of the kids. "I never thought you were afraid of anything, Staci. You're always so cool and . . . well, unfeeling, sort of."

"I am not unfeeling," I hollered. "Just because I refuse to go around letting everyone know exactly what I'm thinking, I get accused of being unfeeling. I hear other kids and how they talk about everyone. I'm not about to risk being the object of a bunch of jokes or rumors."

"You'll miss a lot of good things in life with that attitude," Andy said. "Maybe I spend too much time having a blast in life but I think you don't spend enough. You're always serious and suspicious."

"I'm not the one who's worried about not having made even the most basic plans for my future," I snapped. "It seems to me you should have your own act together before you criticize me."

"You're probably right, Staci. You usually are." He got up and walked slowly to the other end of the attic and before long he was deeply involved in the dragon hunt with Rooster and Beth. I watched them, wondering why I couldn't let myself go like that and just have a good time. I could hear them all laughing as I went back to work on the telescope, diligently stroking back and forth with the coarse sand, following the directions carefully.

The doorbell rang and I sighed with frustration. It was probably Mrs. Warren coming to make sure Andy had delivered the meatloaf and the instructions properly. Wiping my hands on an old towel, I started downstairs with Rooster, Beth, and Andy close behind. When I opened the door this time, B.J. was standing there.

"Hi, Staci," he said. "I came over to tell you I'm sorry about my rotten disposition the other day. I don't know what got into me. Am I forgiven?"

He looked so cute and so sorry that I threw the door wide open and let him in. I could feel a foolish grin frozen on my face and I wondered what Andy would think if he knew just how ridiculous I could be about this good-looking boy standing in my living room.

"Of course I forgive you," I said. "It was just a bad day for us both." I motioned B.J. toward the couch where Beth was already perched. Andy and Rooster were sitting in the two recliners with Andy reading the TV guide to the kids.

"Hey, how you doing, Andy?" B.J. said with a certain lack of enthusiasm as he sauntered to the couch.

Andy seemed just as unimpressed by the chance meeting. "Fine, B.J. How's your summer been?"

"Great. I'm getting in a lot of star gazing and I work for a few hours at my uncle's lumber yard every day."

"How's Marlo?" Andy asked. "Still driving

around in that new Trans-Am with her nose in the air?"

B.J. was obviously ruffled. "You never change, do you, Andy? You and your crowd have decided Marlo's a creep just because her dad has money." He sat stiffly on the edge of the cushion and I could see he was already eyeing the front door. This was awful. I didn't want B.J. to leave in an angry huff again today. In fact, I didn't want him to leave at all.

"B.J.," I said. "Can I get you a Coke or something?"

He glanced quickly at Beth and rolled his eyes. She glared back at him and slid quietly off the couch. Then she crawled across the floor and took a seat near Andy's feet.

I didn't wait for an answer. I just hurried to the kitchen and poured five big glasses of Coke, put them on a tray, and carried them to the living room. Rooster was watching B.J. with wary eyes. You could have cut the tension in that room with a knife.

"How are the plans coming for Monday night?" I asked brightly, trying to ease B.J. into a conversation.

"Pretty good," he said. "We're driving all the telescopes out to Mercer Island early in the day so there won't be any temperature or fogging problems when the meeting starts."

"I can hardly wait," I said. "This will be my first chance to observe Venus through a high-powered telescope."

I was trying to ignore Rooster who was

standing up now, still watching B.J. with those wary blue eyes. I wasn't sure but he seemed to be edging closer to the couch. My feet were tapping nervously against the floor as I tried to keep B.J. talking. "How are we all going to get to the island?" I asked.

"Most of the members are meeting at the library. There will be three or four cars going out." His voice had an edge in it that sounded as if he would rather be someplace else, that he was sorry he'd come back to apologize.

"Will you be at the library?"

"No. I'm going to stay out on the island with Marlo and watch the telescopes. We can't leave all that expensive equipment out there with no one to guard it." He was standing up now and I was frantic. As uncomfortable as the whole situation was, I didn't want him to leave.

Then the doorbell rang again. Rooster leaped across the room and pulled the door open. I was trying to beat him to the door, knowing how Dad didn't like the little kids to open it without checking first to see who was there. I almost caught up with him but didn't quite make it. As he opened the door wide, I found myself staring straight into Marlo Cate's eyes.

She was wearing a white sundress and looked gorgeous. But the haughty look on her face hadn't changed a bit. I sucked in my breath, wondering what to do. I didn't have to

make much of a decision since Marlo swept
into the house without even being asked, just
as though she were some kind of royalty or
something.

"B.J.," she gushed. "I thought you might
want to go out to the beach this afternoon. I
couldn't find you but when I stopped at the
Safeway to ask your sister where you were, I
happened to see your car outside."

I wondered how she had managed that little
miracle since our house was several blocks
from the store and not on a major street. I
made a mental note to hate B.J.'s sister if I
ever met her.

"Why don't you come in, Marlo?" I offered
as she sat gracefully down on the couch next
to B.J. "I'm sure I can find some more Coke if
you'd like something to drink."

She just shook her head regally from side to
side while her eyes roamed around the living
room and her lip curled slightly. "What are
you doing here, Andy?" she asked. "I never
think of you as being sociable."

The situation was going from bad to worse.
Rooster was watching everything, taking in
the entire situation as if he were absorbing all
the tension in the room. I sensed trouble in
the air. When Rooster got that look on his
face, usually something dreadful happened—
like the incident with the pail of water.

B.J. stood up again. "Okay, Marlo," he said.
"Going to the beach sounds like a great idea. I

came over to see how Staci was coming on her telescope and to apologize to her brother. I had no idea she'd be so busy." He nodded slightly in Andy's direction. "Let's go."

They were both standing now, and I felt an odd sense of relief . . . until I noticed Rooster ambling slowly back into the living room with poor Harvey draped over one arm, and a glass of Coke balanced in the other.

"Want to see my cat, Marlo?" he asked sweetly. "She's going to have babies any minute."

Marlo backed up, shaking her head vigorously from side to side as if she'd lost her tongue. That gave me a certain satisfaction but, all in all, I could still feel disaster coming. Marlo's legs hit the obstacle of the couch just as Rooster and Harvey hit Marlo.

Amid the tangled heap of arms, legs, and paws on the couch, Marlo was screaming herself into a rage because Harvey was licking her face. Then I noticed a bold, soggy Coke spill on Marlo's sundress. B.J. pulled Marlo to her feet and dragged her toward the door.

"This place is nuts!" he yelled. "I think that kid and that cat ought to be locked up!"

Marlo was sobbing. Andy was laughing and Beth and Rooster were grinning. I wanted to crawl under a rock. The front door slammed before I could tell B.J. and Marlo I was sorry.

As soon as they were gone, hilarity broke out around me.

"Good show, Rooster," Andy snorted. "That stuffy Marlo has had something like that coming for years. Since kindergarten really."

I was furious. "How dare you!" I yelled at Andy. "How dare you encourage my brother in that kind of behavior! I don't care what you think about Marlo, she didn't deserve that." I turned to my brother. "And don't try to tell me you didn't know Harvey would jump out of your arms. She does it almost every time you pick her up these days."

Beth was sitting on the floor stroking the cat's head. "You care more about that dumb old girl than you do about Harvey, Staci. She might be ready to have her babies."

"No chance," I yelled. "She's going to stay pregnant forever just so she can jump on my friends and humiliate me every few days. I wish I were an only child!" I stalked into the kitchen and started slamming things around. As I cleaned up the mess from the Cokes I saw another puddle of Coke on the floor.

Andy followed me to the kitchen. "Don't get so upset, Staci," he said. "Life is too beautiful to waste it worrying about little things like a cat and a Coke landing on Marlo Cate." He bent down and wiped up the Coke off the floor. "Life is too short to spend a lot of time trying to please people like Marlo."

"Who has time to worry about pleasing her?" I was thinking about Andy's statement that life was beautiful.

"Let me go get the rest of the glasses out of the living room for you," Andy said. "I'll be glad to wash them."

"Go home, Andy. Just go home and keep your theories about life and beauty to yourself. Maybe your life is terrific. Maybe nothing ever goes wrong for you. But you don't have to live with Rooster every day and you don't have to live without a mother." I just wanted this day to be over, this whole summer to be over. From the conversation I'd heard when B.J. first arrived, I could safely assume that B.J. and Marlo were both students at the high school where I would be enrolled next fall. I could also safely assume that my social life was destroyed before I even went for the first day. I could just hear Marlo telling everyone there how my cat and my brother had ruined her beautiful dress and how my brother had dumped a pail of water on B.J.

Just great, I seethed, as I stomped around the kitchen. I haven't even had half a chance and already I'm an outcast.

"You really want me to leave?" Andy asked. He was leaning against the back door looking at me with confusion. "You honestly believe Marlo is worth all this anguish?"

"Yes," I screamed. "I think she is and so is B.J. They were my friends and now I doubt if they'll ever speak to me again."

"Big loss," Andy muttered as he slowly opened the door. "Just remember one thing,

Staci. Marlo Cate doesn't have any real friends. The only people she cares about are those with enough prestige to help her social life. And B.J.'s not much better. At least he's not when it comes to Marlo. He thinks she's God's gift to mankind and he never gets upset when she crushes some poor slob's feelings or pulls one of her high and mighty acts like she did on you in your own house." Andy glared. "You may have your future all mapped out, Staci. But you don't have much judgment."

"I do so!" I was slamming dishes around and turning on the oven to start dinner.

"No, Staci. You don't. You'll let her say anything she wants to you if you can just keep hanging around with her and B.J. I think you're changing. You're so lonesome since you had to move up here that you don't care about real people anymore." He was glaring at me. "There was a time, Staci, when you would have defended your brother and told someone like Marlo just where to get off. Now," he said, shaking his head, "I don't think you care about anything except making new friends no matter what it costs you."

The door closed quietly behind him just as I stuck the meatloaf in the oven. I tried not to think about the things he had said but they kept playing through my mind like a record that gets stuck in one groove and says the same thing over and over again.

Was Andy right? Had I changed? I couldn't

believe it. Even if I hated Marlo Cate, I would
feel sorry for her if a kid ruined her dress. And
B.J.? Did I really care more for him than I did
Andy or the kids? My mind whirled with
questions until I was too confused to think
anymore and I went in search of the kids.

I found them up in Beth's room. They were
sitting on the floor playing checkers. Neither
of them spoke to me when I walked in. "Hey,
you guys," I said. "What's going on here?"

Rooster glared at me. "I don't like you anymore, Staci. You were mean to me and Beth
and Andy. You let that dumb girl say nasty
things about Andy and you didn't even yell at
her or B.J." He moved a checker and studied
the board, apparently finished with his
speech.

"Is that how you feel, Beth?"

"Yes. You chose that girl over Harvey." Her
eyes were wide and brimming with tears. "I
don't know why you don't like Harvey, Staci.
Our family gets lonely sometimes and I think
we should all stick together. Why don't you
think that?"

"I do, Beth. I really do." I got down on the
floor with them but both of them edged away.
"Why can't you two see that I need friends like
everyone else? I can't just keep hanging
around here all day every day and never make
friends of my own."

"What's the matter with Andy?" Rooster
asked, his face all contorted like he was about

to cry. "Andy is a good friend but you never like to sit around and talk to him."

"I do too, Rooster. Just not all the time." I put my arm on his shoulder. "We talked today for a long time. But it's not the same. I've known Andy all my life. He's a different kind of friend."

"What kind?" Rooster asked, pulling away again.

I just sat there trying to figure out how I should answer that question. What kind of friend was Andy? He was an old friend, the kind you take for granted if you're not careful. But he wasn't the kind of friend I would have picked on my own. He had just sort of always been there and he would probably always be here in the future, playing some dumb game with Rooster and Beth and showing up every time I turned around.

"What kind of friend?" Beth prompted. "Why don't you answer?"

"Because I'm not sure I can," I snapped. "If you two want to go on thinking I hate Harvey and hate this family, just go ahead. You're only mad at me because I want some friends of my own, people who weren't inherited from Grandpa like this house." I jumped up and ran downstairs to check on dinner.

While I was setting the table my dad came in from work. He looked tired when he walked into the kitchen and sat down.

"How was your day, princess?" he asked.

"Have you worked out a schedule where you can work on your telescope yet?"

"Sort of." I stirred a pot of green beans and tried to think of some way to tell him how confusing things kept getting here at home during the day. But he probably wouldn't understand. Dad's idea for solving any problem was to "organize." If one was really organized, one could make extra minutes and hours in any day. I wondered just how well my father would handle the crazy things that went on around here while he was gone.

"That meatloaf smells delicious, Staci. You're finally starting to get the hang of your domestic duties."

I glanced at him. "I didn't make the meatloaf, Dad. Mrs. Warren sent it over with Andy this morning."

"Well, wasn't that thoughtful?"

"Maybe it was, Dad. But I would rather do the cooking myself." I put the lid back down on the beans and started cutting up a cucumber for the salad. "I hate it when I have to take her dishes back and she offers to do everything around here."

"Aren't you being pretty hard on her, Staci?"

"I had a mother once," I tried to explain as calmly as possible. "I don't need Andy's mother to try to pretend that she's going to take Mom's place."

He stood up, came across the room and put

his arms around me. "Hey, princess. Don't get so upset. If you want to do all the cooking, just think of a nice way to tell her to stop."

I tore lettuce into a bowl with dismay. Dad was doing it again. I'd mentioned mother and he was telling me to be nice when I told Mrs. Warren not to cook any more meals for us. What would it take to get my father to talk about Mom to us kids? I remembered the talk I had with Rooster and Beth. Did I want to go through that again? Yes, I decided, I did if it meant that Dad would talk to us, really talk to us and quit pretending that Mom was just out of town on business.

My father didn't seem to notice my mood. He picked up the evening paper and opened it to the sports section. The discussion was over before it had even begun. I went to the bottom of the stairs and called the kids for dinner. This was one time, even though I hated to admit it, that I was glad for Mrs. Warren's help with dinner.

We had finished dinner and the kids were helping me carry the dishes to the sink when the phone rang. My father answered it in the den and I could hear his voice booming through the house. "Staci," he bellowed. "It's for you. A young man."

I wanted to crawl inside the dishwasher. I didn't care who was on the phone, I didn't want to talk to anyone who had heard my father trumpet out the news that it was a young man as if that was such a rare happening it was worthy of hats and horns.

"Staci," Beth said. "Dad says there's a boy on the phone for you."

"I heard him," I muttered.

"It's probably that icky B.J.," Rooster said. That thought hadn't occurred to me and new panic boiled inside. B.J. was the one person I'd most hate to have heard my father's remarks.

"Staci," Dad yelled again. "There's a young fellow on the phone and he wants to talk to you."

I threw my dishtowel on the kitchen counter and slunk toward the den and my doom. The only person who would possibly understand was Andy and after the way I'd treated him this afternoon, I doubted whether he would call. Besides, Dad knew Andy's voice and Andy never bothered to call. He just leaped the hedgerow between our houses and came crashing over whenever he had something to say.

When I got to the phone I looked at it as if it were a living enemy. My father thrust it into my hand and wandered back to his chair by the TV. I put the receiver to my ear. "Hello?"

"Staci? This is B.J."

My insides flipped over about four times. "Uh huh," I said idiotically. "This is Staci."

"I know," B.J. said. "I wondered if I could try to make up to you one more time for what happened today. I'm sure you were at a loss when Marlo popped in and I know you had nothing to do with what your brother did."

"Make up how?"

"Well, I was thinking we might play miniature golf or go to a movie. Would you like that?"

Would I like it? The understatement of the year! "I'll have to ask," I mumbled. "What time would you want to go?"

"I don't know. About seven if that's okay."

"Let me find out." I put the phone against my hip. "Dad?"

He looked up and smiled. "Is that the young man from your astronomy club?"

I nodded. "He wants me to go to a movie or play putt-putt. Can I?" I asked, shaking my head vigorously to indicate that I wanted my father to say no. He must have thought I had a nervous tic or something because he just grinned.

"I don't see why not," he boomed. "Just so you're in by eleven."

I put the phone back to my ear. "Dad says that will be fine if I'm home by eleven. Is that too early?"

"No problem," B.J. said. "I've got to work tomorrow. I'll pick you up at seven then, Staci. Bye."

"Bye," I answered and hung the phone up quickly before some other catastrophe could occur. One thing B.J. had said was correct. My home was a crazy place. And it was rapidly driving me crazy too.

I heard Rooster and Beth fighting in the kitchen and went to break up the battle just as a spoon or something fell to the floor with a clang. Another full-filled evening in the life of the Callahan family, I thought grimly, as I hurried around the corner.

4

I spent the next hour and a half experimenting with make-up and trying to decide what to wear. I was sitting at the little stool in front of my mirror gazing at freckles and applying black mascara. I did all right with the top lashes but when I touched the wand to the bottom lashes, I stuck it in my eye accidently and ended up with a huge black smudge. By the time I removed the mess with cold cream, my cheekbone was red and I had rubbed my eye a little too hard.

My corn-flake-colored hair looked passable though. I had brushed it till it shone.

Beth came in and sat down on the end of my bed, watching me as if I'd suddenly changed, sprouted wings or something. "Are you excited, Staci?" she asked, her eyes sparkling.

"A little," I mumbled. "I wish I knew how to put on make-up, Beth. I want to cover my freckles and look pretty like Marlo and I can't even put mascara on my lashes."

Beth stared with that star-struck look. "I think you're very beautiful, Staci. That's why that Marlo girl was so mean. Because she's jealous."

"Jealous? Anybody who looks like Marlo Cate doesn't have to be jealous of any girl in the world."

Beth shook her head. "I think you're wrong, Staci. Next to you, Marlo looks like a plastic flower, one that's fake and hard." She smiled. "You look like a rose to me, Staci. A real pretty rose that's not plastic or anything. Just real."

I got up from the stool, walked over, and hugged my little sister around the neck. She'd made me feel much better. I went back to the mirror and applied just a touch of blush and lipstick. That was all the make-up I usually wore and I was ashamed of myself for trying to look like Marlo. I was Staci Callahan. Nothing more. If that wasn't enough for B.J. then he could take Marlo on his next date.

I had just finished brushing my hair one last time, fluffing it and liking the way it curled around my shoulders, when I heard the doorbell ring. The thought that my father might answer the bell brought me to my feet in a hurry and I ran toward the stairs like crazy.

I was too late. I reached the first landing in

time to hear my father boom, "Well, young fellow, you must be P.J.!"

"B.J., sir," B.J. said. "My name is B.J. Keller . . . I met Staci at the astronomy club at the library."

"Isn't that nice?" Dad said. "I'm glad you young folks have such healthy interests. Not like some of these hippie types I see downtown."

Hippie types! Nobody had said that for years. B.J. probably thought my father was as crazy as Rooster. I huddled on the top step, around the corner where Dad and B.J. couldn't see me. I wanted to stay there forever. Never go down again, even to eat. Beth gave me a strange look and left.

"Staci?" Dad called. "Your young man is here. Better get a move on."

I heard B.J. cough politely and ask about the weather. But my father was not about to be deterred from his task of seeing his oldest daughter off on her first date. "Where's that sister of yours?" he asked Beth.

"Sitting on the top step," my traitorous sister said.

Dad roared. "Isn't that just like a woman? She probably doesn't want to appear too eager for her first date." His hearty laugh echoed through the whole house, as I rose and stumbled down the stairs.

B.J. looked up as I turned the corner. His face broke out in a nervous smile of relief.

Rooster was perched on the bottom step holding Harvey and I could imagine the trauma B.J. had endured as he'd stood trapped between the cat, my prankster brother, and jolly old Dad.

"There's our princess now," Dad said, not at all distressed by the painful look on my face or the strained look in B.J.'s eyes. "Isn't she a beauty?"

B.J. nodded and I smiled grimly, feeling my teeth go dry and my top lip stick to them as if my smile were a frozen thing that would never go away.

"I'm ready," I mumbled.

"Don't you think you better take a sweater?" my father asked, already pulling my old blue cardigan off the coat hook by the door. I snatched the awful thing from his hands, muttered something that sounded like goodbye, and stumbled out the door with B.J.

We hurried toward his car, a late model Cutlass. We were three blocks down the street before B.J. spoke. "Your dad's really interesting," he said.

"Yeah."

He smiled and patted my hand. "Hey, don't let it get you down. You should hear my dad when my sister's dates come by. Sometimes I think she'll become a nun just to avoid those meetings at the front door."

That made me laugh and I threw the sweater in the back seat and relaxed a little. "Your dad does things like that? Honest?"

"He sure does. I think it's a special course they all take on communicating with anyone under the age of twenty."

I laughed again. "I'm just glad it's over with. And, B.J., I'm sorry about earlier today, the things with my brother and Marlo."

"That's all right. It didn't kill her." He laughed. "That's probably the first time she's gotten her dress dirty in seventeen years."

I felt my cheeks flush as I remembered the scene with Harvey and Marlo. "But still, B.J. That was an awful thing to happen to any girl."

"Like I said, she'll live."

"But I'll bet she never speaks to me again."

"You may be right. It will be a while before she does."

"But won't you be going to the same high school as Andy and me?"

He looked at me quizzically. "Yeah. So what difference does that make?"

"And Marlo?" I asked. "Does she go to the same school?"

B.J. nodded slowly, as if for the first time it had occurred to him that Marlo could destroy me socially. "I see," he said. "This could be quite a problem unless we get Marlo to change her opinion of you before September. She's just about the most popular senior girl."

"That figures," I said. "All she has to do is tell the other girls about my weird brother and I'll feel like an outcast after the first day."

"Oh, come on. It won't be as bad as all that.

I've got a lot of friends at the school. So does old Andy for that matter." He grinned and his blue eyes were as blue as Puget Sound.

On both sides of us there were tall pine trees, their beauty reflected in the water. Suddenly I felt good again. B.J.'s father said embarrassing things, too. Probably all fathers did that. I leaned back in the seat and smiled. I was on a date, a real date, and the guy I was with was the most handsome boy I'd ever met.

"So," B.J. said. "Do you want to try a movie or a couple games of putt-putt?"

"Putt-putt, I think. I used to really enjoy that when we lived in Federal Way. I haven't played in quite a while now."

"Federal Way? Somehow I thought you'd moved here from a long way off. How come your family decided to locate in Seattle?"

My hands knotted for a moment. Questions like this always seemed to lead to more and more questions. But there was no law that said I had to tell everything. "Oh," I said lightly. "After my grandfather died we just decided to move back to Mom's childhood home. That house has been in our family for more than forty years and we're pretty sentimental about it."

"That's great," B.J. said as he negotiated a wide curve in the road. "I never have known that kind of roots. My dad's folks live in California and my mom's folks are in Wisconsin. I've lived in four states in my life. When my dad got out of the Air Force he decided

Washington was a good place to settle down, so we moved here when I was in the ninth grade."

"I never moved in my life," I said. "Except for this time. I think I'd hate moving around a lot."

"You get used to it." B.J. was pulling into the parking lot at the putt-putt course and I was sorry. I had enjoyed our talk. It was kind of special to share personal things with someone as terrific as him.

He went up to the window and paid, got our putters and our cards. The evening air felt cool and refreshing on my arms, and I was so happy to be with B.J. I didn't care anymore if Marlo was rude to me at astronomy club. We'd get to be good friends after school started and she'd get to know me better. I even had to stop myself from grinning like a fool as B.J. came walking back toward me.

"Okay, Staci. Let's just see how coordinated you are." B.J. smiled and bowed, indicating I was to take the first shot.

I shrugged my shoulders slightly. "Remember. I said I hadn't played in quite a while." I leaned over the ball, took careful aim and swung. I watched, pleased as the ball went up and over the little wooden obstacle, rolled down the other side, rimmed the cup, and dropped in. "A hole in one," I yelled, jumping up and down.

"Great," B.J. said.

His ball didn't clear the obstacle on the first

try. It did on the second but the ball didn't go in the cup. And that was sort of how the whole game went. I couldn't seem to do anything wrong and he couldn't make any shots, even the easy ones. B.J. was smiling but his face kept looking tighter and tighter around the mouth and eyes. I stopped leaping around when I made a good shot. I'd just stand there and shrug my shoulders as if I had no idea how I could be having such good luck.

We only played one game. As soon as it was over, B.J. grabbed my putter and steered me toward the window of the office. "These greens are in rotten shape," he said. "Almost impossible to play scientifically. Watching the angle and all that."

"I know," I said. "I just got lucky." I wanted to get out of there, go have a Coke or something and talk about astronomy. Talk about anything except this game.

B.J. drove straight to a drive-in restaurant without even asking me first. "What would you like?" he asked.

"Just a large Coke. I'm thirsty."

When our drinks came he leaned back in the seat, looked at me and smiled. "Tell me, Staci. How can you be such a capable athlete and not have the discipline to work on your telescope more often?"

I looked at him with surprise. "B.J., I've worked on it quite a bit this week. At least with everything considered. I knew when I started it that it might take a year or more to finish."

"A year?"

"Yeah. I plan to get a job when school starts so I can save money for college. But I'll still work on it as often as I can. And I always have a lot of time on weekends."

"I still wonder if you're serious. I finished mine in less than five months. It takes self-discipline to make yourself work on it every day."

"I know that, B.J. But I have quite a bit of responsibility at home though and I can't just work straight through the way you probably did. You've met my little brother and sister. Do you think you could take care of them all day and still finish a telescope in less than five months?"

He looked at me. "I don't think you should have to take care of them. You're only going to be sixteen one time in your life. I'm sorry if I'm butting into something that's none of my business but you didn't have those kids and I think your folks should make other arrangements and let you have a life of your own."

"I'm getting paid for watching them this summer," I snapped. "I told you I'm working to save money for college." I wondered how B.J. could be so insensitive. But I hadn't told him about my mother and he had no way of knowing.

"I told you it was none of my business," B.J.

said, setting the Coke cups outside on a shelf and starting the car. "I didn't mean to upset you, Staci. It's just that you'll only have this one chance. You can get a scholarship or a government loan to help out when it's time for college. You don't have to have every cent saved up."

"I know, B.J. But I feel I should save as much as I can."

"I just hope you don't regret all the years that you'll miss out on having a good time with other kids and doing things for yourself."

"I'm not sure I have a whole lot of choice."

He was driving back toward my house and I hated to see the evening end. It had been an incredible mixture of up and down feelings but all in all it hadn't been bad for a first date.

We pulled up in front of my house and I noticed the porch light was on and also the living room light. B.J. turned off the motor and put his arm around me. He looked across the hedge at Andy's house. "I meant to ask you how you got tied up with old Andy Warren. He's a little strange, don't you think?"

I thought of all the times I'd felt the same way about Andy as I'd watched him crawl around the floor setting up intricate race sets with Rooster. But in spite of all that, I felt defensive. "Andy's all right," I said. "I've known him since before we started kindergarten."

"Yeah? Well, maybe I just don't know him well enough."

He looked up at the sky through the windshield glass. "It's not a very good night for star-gazing," he sighed.

"No, I guess not."

I felt B.J.'s arm tighten around my shoulders and I looked up to see him leaning toward me. His eyes were a soft blue in the darkness, and I felt as though I could gaze into them forever. As he leaned closer, I closed my eyes and felt B.J.'s lips touch mine.

The whole thing was wonderful. I wanted B.J. Keller to go on kissing me forever. His mouth was warm and firm and I loved the way our lips felt together. My mind raced with thoughts of seeing him again in the future. Maybe dates on the beach where we would run toward each other in slow motion like in that commercial and he would sweep me up in the air and whirl me around, pledging his undying love.

The kiss ended. B.J. smiled, got out of the car, and came around to my side. He opened the door and stood back so I could get out. He had his arm lightly around my waist as we walked toward my front door. I wanted to stop and hug him right there under the street lights. B.J. had kissed me and everything was going to be wonderful.

As we walked up the steps, my father pulled the front door open and stuck his head outside. "Oh, there you two are. I was starting to worry."

"What time is it, Dad? Is it after eleven?"

"Oh, no. I don't think so. I just got concerned and thought I'd take a look and see if you'd gotten back."

B.J. had pulled his hand away the moment the door opened. Now he was backing down the walk and waving at me. "See you Monday, Staci," he said. "Glad to have met you, Mr. Callahan."

I hurried upstairs and got undressed for bed, thinking all the time about the soft and wonderful feeling of the kiss. I had been kissed a few other times at parties and stuff but never like this, never with a guy I liked so much and never in a car while I was on a date.

It seemed as though I had just crawled into bed and drifted off when I felt someone shaking my shoulder. I opened my eyes and I could barely make out Beth's features in the dark. "Staci," she whispered. "Wake up! Harvey's on my bed and she's acting funny."

I figured it must be time for the kittens to be born and, groaning a little, I rolled out of bed and followed Beth down the hall. Rooster was already in the room, curled up on the end of the bed with Harvey and crooning senselessly in her face.

Harvey really did look sick. She was limp, her sides were heaving and her eyes had a glazed look. I'd never seen a cat have kittens before but I had a feeling this wasn't the way it should look. I stroked her soft head and heard myself crooning just as senselessly as Rooster had done.

"Go get a bowl of water, Beth," I whispered. "And try not to wake Dad up unless I decide we have to."

She hurried out and Rooster started rocking back and forth on the bed. "Is she going to be all right, Staci?" he asked. I looked up and saw the terror in his eyes and for the first time in my life realized how much my brother cared about this cat.

Fiercely, I wanted this cat to be all right. I wanted her to be more than all right. I wanted her to produce a litter of fine healthy kittens for Rooster and Beth to watch her feed and love.

Beth came back with the water and I made Harvey get up and drink a little of it. Then her sides heaved a bit more and I got really scared. What could I do? I remembered Andy and how good he'd always been with Harvey and every other animal that had passed through our two houses over the years. "Stay here," I whispered to the kids. "I'm going to run and get Andy. Just sit with Harvey and be quiet until I get back."

The trip down the stairs was tricky because Dad's bedroom was on the first floor and the steps were practically over his head. I went down slowly, feeling the steps first to see if they were going to creak. When I got to the bottom I hurried to the back door, pulled it open and ran like crazy across the wide green lawns. I was wearing pajamas. Years of practice had trained me to jump the hedge.

Soon I had shinnied up the old oak tree outside Andy's window and I was tapping softly on the glass. Nothing happened and I tapped again. Finally he came to the window. He looked a little scared as he peeked out through his curtain and I giggled. "What do you want, Staci?" he asked after he'd raised the glass.

"It's Harvey," I whispered. "She's acting weird. Not like she's having the kittens but like she's sick."

He disappeared for a minute and then he was back, dressed in his pajama top and a pair of jeans. I steadied the big limb as Andy climbed out the window and then we hurried down the tree and across to my house. Getting in was easy but we had a couple of scares going up the steps. All of them seemed creaky.

Soon we were in Beth's room and Andy was looking at Harvey. "I think she's all right," he said. "And I don't think it's quite time for the kittens. Did she drink water for you?"

"A little," I said.

"I think we should take her outside for a few minutes. Let her walk around and get some fresh air. Eat a little grass if she wants." He grinned. "I think this cat can suffer from morning sickness at any hour of the day."

Rooster and Beth wouldn't hear of being left behind so all four of us snuck down the stairs.

Andy carried Harvey carefully, hoping to get her outside before she got sick.

I looked at the clock on the kitchen wall as we hurried through. It was two A.M. I was surprised. I must have slept longer than I thought.

The air outside was marvelous. The sky had cleared and I could see several of my favorite constellations. Andy and I flopped down on the grass and he let Harvey go so she could wander around and start feeling better. I knew she wouldn't go far. She never left the backyard, and in her present condition, I was sure she'd stay close.

Rooster and Beth hurried over to their swing set and started to play in the clear moonlight. The magic of doing something different, something we weren't supposed to do, was getting to all of us. I felt free and happy. Andy didn't seem upset that I'd wakened him in the middle of the night to take a look at a cat. He didn't even seem mad about the argument we'd had earlier.

"This is fun," I whispered.

"It is, kind of. If my mom looked in my room right now and saw me missing, she'd have four hundred police officers, the national guard, and twelve scout troops combing the neighborhood before we could holler across the yard and tell her we were fine."

I laughed. "So would my dad."

"You went out with B.J. tonight, didn't you?"

I nodded. "How did you know?"

"Oh, I saw you going out to his car with him. Did you have fun?"

"I guess so," I said. "We just played putt-putt."

"I'll bet you beat him," Andy said.

"Yeah, I did, but how did you know?"

"Don't you remember that time your grandfather drove us down and we played a few games? You whipped me every time."

I smiled. I had forgotten that day. Grandpa Barclay had been crazy about Andy. He had called and asked if I'd come in for the weekend and I'd agreed. That day had been only three or four months after Mom died and I'd hit that little golf ball with all the fury in my fourteen-year-old body, knocking the ball around that course the way I'd wanted to strike out at the doctors and everyone else that I'd somehow believed should have saved my mother's life.

I wasn't sure that day who had comforted whom, me, Grandpa or Andy. I liked Andy. I really did. Every time I needed a friend to talk to or a shoulder to cry on, Andy was there.

Harvey wandered back toward us and she was obviously feeling much better. She rubbed her head against Andy's legs and I could hear her purring from two feet away. "That's one thing you could do with your life, Andy," I said. "You could be a vet. You're really terrific with animals."

He smiled slowly and in the moonlight his

eyes sparkled like diamonds. His mouth crinkled with that special laughter he usually kept inside. "I just might do that, Staci. You're right. I love animals and my grades are pretty good now." He patted Harvey's head. "The only way I can fail is if they check my records and find out I was a first-grade failure. And there are a couple of people, Marlo Cate included, who like to remind me every so often that I should be a senior next year."

"Forget her." I grinned. "If she gets out of line again all we'll have to do is aim Rooster and Harvey at her and she'll probably leave town."

Andy laughed so hard that the kids came running over to see what was going on. "Come on, you two," I said. "The crisis is over. Harvey's not having kittens tonight and she's not sick anymore." I stood up. "Thanks, Andy, for all the help. Don't fall going back in your window."

"I won't." He grinned. "Good-night."

We watched him run across the yard and jump the hedge before the three of us hurried into the house with Harvey. We didn't get caught going up the stairs and soon I had both kids tucked back in bed.

I was exhausted but happy as I climbed into my own bed. The comfortable old brass bed that had belonged to my grandparents seemed to become more my own with every day that passed.

I closed my eyes and tried to think of B.J.'s

kiss as I drifted off to sleep. But Andy's face kept intruding on the vision and at last I gave up and let him stay. I imagined Andy Warren as he would look in a white coat doctoring sick animals and cheering their owners up with funny stories.

5

Saturday morning I got up earlier than usual and went straight to the attic as soon as I was dressed. I pulled open the two large windows at the end of the room and breathed the fresh air that was blowing in off the Sound, brushing the pines as it swept toward me. Soon the whole attic smelled clean and woodsy.

The sun had just come up over Mount Ranier and I could see the dazzling peak in the distance, standing tall and majestic against the eastern horizon. My heart was full and overflowing.

Harvey was still all right. She had rubbed my legs and purred while I fed her this morning. Andy wasn't mad anymore. And most of all, my heart sang, B.J. Keller had taken me on a date and he had kissed me good-night.

The work on the telescope went fast. By
eight-thirty, when Dad and the kids were up
and around and I went downstairs to have
some breakfast, I had gotten more accomplished than in all my previous efforts put
together. Maybe if I really stuck with it today,
I could catch up on all the time I'd lost early in
the week.

Dad looked up as I entered the kitchen.
"Well, hello, sleepyhead. I didn't think you
were going to get up today."

"I've been up for hours," I smiled. "Already
finished my first step of grinding, I think."

"Good for you." He was standing at the
stove making omelets and the smell of siz-
zling bacon and brewing coffee filled the
kitchen. I watched him and thought how cute
he looked in the silly old lace-trimmed apron
of grandma's that he had tied around his
waist. I gave him a quick hug, then snitched a
piece of bacon.

"Can we go swimming today?" Beth asked.
"Will you take us down to the pool, Dad?"

"Sorry, Beth, but I can't. I've got a lot of
paperwork to do this weekend." Dad carried a
large omelet to the table and cut it in half for
the kids. "Maybe you can talk Staci into taking you."

I glanced at my father quickly, fearful of
losing another day of work when I wasn't even
being paid to watch the kids. B.J.'s words
about too much responsibility played through

my mind. "Dad," I stammered. "I want to work on my telescope today."

"Oh, please, Staci," Beth begged. "We can have fun."

"No," I yelled.

I looked across the table at Rooster. He was gazing at me with tears brimming in his huge blue eyes and his lower lip was trembling.

"Staci," Dad said. "If you'll take them to the pool for a while after lunch, I'll straighten the kitchen and you can work upstairs all morning."

I nodded, knowing the battle was lost. In my mind I could see myself sitting in front of some military officer in a future interview with NASA and hear the man telling me that I couldn't possibly qualify as an astronaut because I hadn't even been able to finish a simple telescope project when I was in high school.

The rest of the morning wasn't too productive even though I stayed in the attic and tried very hard to get some work done. The kids made at least twelve trips up there asking me if it was time to go yet. And twice my father called me downstairs to ask where I kept things in the kitchen.

At eleven-thirty I gave up. Rooster was whining for a sandwich and I knew it was almost time to go anyway. So we ate a light lunch and then changed into our swimsuits and started for the pool.

The kids danced around me, swinging their towels as we walked. It was a pretty day and I didn't really mind taking a break to go swimming once we got away from the house. When I had been in junior high in Federal Way, I had almost decided to try out for the swim team. But astronomy had been my first love and I didn't have time to devote the necessary dedication to both interests so I had chosen astronomy. Still, I knew I was an excellent swimmer and the thought of losing myself in the pool for an hour or so, racing through the cool water, seemed very appealing.

I had to hold Rooster back when we got to the pool. He tried to run through the turnstile before I'd paid our money. But at last we were motioned through by a boy with red hair like Rooster's and I let the kids go. They were pretty good swimmers themselves, having taken lessons since they were about four, and there were two lifeguards on duty just in case.

I threw my towel in a corner by the fence and sat down to put suntan lotion on my shoulders and arms. Even though I had freckles, I usually got a dark tan every summer. That was the only time I really liked the way my skin looked, right at the end of August when it was time for school and I could apply a bit of blush and lipstick and look better than a lot of girls who wore tons of make-up.

It was several minutes before I was ready to go in the water. I headed for the high diving board, anxious to spring into the air and do a good dive before slicing through the cool water and doing several laps back and forth across the pool.

Just as I walked out on the diving board, I saw B.J. and Marlo coming through the turn-stile. My breath caught in my throat. Why was he with her? After all, last night he had been with me and even kissed me good-night. B.J. looked up, saw me and pointed. Marlo fol-lowed his gaze and I was so unnerved that I dove before I was ready, landing in a belly flop.

The stinging flesh on my stomach was noth-ing compared to the humiliation I felt. My skin felt hot under the surface of the water and I dog-paddled toward the opposite side of the pool from where B.J. and Marlo were. I knew I must look like a total, untrained nov-ice as I struggled up the side and headed for my towel. That thought made me even more angry at myself. I probably swam much better than Marlo, better than B.J., too.

I flopped down on the towel and covered my head with my shirt as if I were sleeping, just lying there getting a tan and completely un-aware that B.J. and Marlo had walked in. I had been lying there for about five minutes when I sensed someone standing near my head. I tried to ignore the feeling, hoping whoever it was would go away.

"Staci?" It was Marlo.

I didn't move a muscle.

"Staci, that is you, isn't it?"

I lifted one corner of my T-shirt and looked at her. She was wearing a cranberry-colored bikini and her skin was toasted a gorgeous bronze. I remembered her saying that her family had a pool. So why was she here, I wondered. "Oh, Marlo," I said, trying to look as if she'd just wakened me. "How are you?"

"Just fine. You sure can go to sleep in a hurry. I saw your dive a few minutes ago. You need to work on your form."

"I was just fooling around for my little brother," I lied.

Marlo's head turned quickly and she scanned the pool. "Is he here?"

I nodded.

"I don't like to be nasty, Staci, but I think your brother is a creep. I came over to make sure you were still planning to come out to the island Monday night." She gazed at me coldly. "You won't have to haul your little family along, will you?"

"I'm sure not, Marlo. For some reason my brother doesn't like you any more than you like him."

Marlo stared at me with black eyes that seemed as cold as onyx. "I really couldn't care less about that, Staci. I'm trying to be nice to you because B.J. says you're lonely. Just moving here and all. I understand he took you to play a little game of miniature golf last night because he felt sorry for you."

I felt my cheeks burn with rage. B.J. had only taken me out because he felt sorry for me? He had hurried right to Marlo to tell her all the details. He had probably told her about the kiss too, a kiss for the lonely little girl who had just gone on her first date.

"Please go away, Marlo," I said. "And don't worry. I'll be at the club meeting Monday night. Astronomy is not a hobby for me. It's part of my preparation for the future. There are some interesting kids in that club and I'm not going to let you run me off too easily."

"Why, Staci. I wouldn't think of running you off. You're the most . . . interesting individual we've had come to the club in ages. B.J. and I get such a kick out of some of the things you say and do."

"If you don't mind, I'm trying to get a tan and I don't have much time. I need to get back and work on my telescope."

"If you don't have much time," she said, smiling sweetly, "you should work on your diving form. It's pretty bad, kid."

I rolled over, turned my back on her and tried to ignore the fact that she was there. Pretty soon I sensed her walking away. I got up slowly and walked toward the high diving board again. Unfortunately, B.J. and Marlo were going to be a part of my life for the next year at least. If I stayed out of the pool today, I would spend the whole year dodging them. I wasn't exactly sure what I needed to prove but

I couldn't slink away just because Marlo and B.J. had shown up at the city pool.

I made three or four near perfect dives. I could see B.J. watching me and his expression was becoming more admiring with each dive. The fifth time I climbed to the top of the board, I saw Marlo standing with a group of girls. She was pointing at me and they were all watching and laughing as if Marlo had just told them something hilarious. I glared at her and dove again, feeling the perfection of the dive as I sliced cleanly into the water and slowly stroked toward the edge of the pool.

When I pulled myself up and over the side, I heard a big commotion down at the shallow end. I looked and one of the lifeguards had Rooster by the arm, hollering at him. Then I saw Marlo climb out of the pool. Her lovely hair was drenched and she was holding her arm at a funny angle.

B.J. was motioning at me and I could see his jaw was set in a hard line. It didn't take much of a genius to figure out what had happened. My little brother had shoved Marlo Cate into the pool.

Beth was standing behind Rooster and the lifeguard and she was crying. Beth never cried unless she was really scared so I hurried faster, trying to get there and save my brother and sister from the furious mob.

"Is this your brother, miss?" the lifeguard asked as I walked up.

I nodded. "What happened?"

"He broke one of our strictest rules and pushed this girl in the water. She fell in the shallow end and she could have been seriously injured."

I looked at Marlo, who was crying and holding her arm. Her mascara was smeared all over her cheeks and she really looked awful. She glared at me. "Your brother is a public menace, Staci. I think he should be locked away before he kills someone."

Rooster was looking at me with the same terrified look he'd had the day the pail of water crashed down on B.J.'s head. "Staci," he stammered. "She was talking about you to those other girls." Tears were spilling from his eyes. "She said terrible things, and when I told her not to do it anymore, she called me a jerk."

Beth stood behind Rooster nodding her head. "That's true, Staci," she said. "Marlo said real mean things and she did call Rooster a jerk."

"No matter what," the lifeguard said. "I'm going to have to ask you to take this little boy out of the pool. And I don't want him back here for a week. After that, he'll be on probation. One more incident like this and I'll expel him for the entire summer."

"He needs to be expelled from the human race," Marlo snapped. She was still holding her arm, but I could tell by the white marks around her fingers that she was forcing her arm into the unusual position and I knew it wasn't broken. A broken arm would have been much too painful to twist that way.

I grabbed Rooster's hand and walked toward the exit. Beth followed behind us and we were out on the street heading for home before I could get the kids to stop crying.

"It's all right, Rooster," I said. "She's not hurt. She's just faking, I can tell."

"You should have heard what she said about you, Staci," Rooster said, sniffing and wiping his nose across his arm. "Why did she have to be so mean?"

"She's just a mean girl, Rooster. She wants to make sure that I don't have any friends when school starts next fall. She was just getting an early start on her campaign to ruin my reputation." I remembered all those girls who had been laughing with Marlo and wondered how I had failed to see Rooster. He must have been behind them.

Rooster's actions had been wrong and I knew it. But had Marlo's been right? No. She got exactly what she deserved and the only one who paid was my little brother. I vowed then and there that I would not let Marlo Cate run me off. Not from the astronomy club or from going to school in a few weeks with a positive attitude. There had to be kids who wouldn't believe her stories, kids who would want to get to know me before they made up their minds.

We didn't hurry as we walked home. I was in no mood to explain the whole story to Dad. He loved us but he was the kind of father who never wanted us to make waves. The first thing he would say if he knew about the incident at the pool was how impulsively Rooster had acted and didn't he know he could have hurt that girl?

I had taken money to buy the kids an ice cream bar at the pool, so we stopped at a snow cone stand on the way home. Rooster wouldn't order anything because he was feeling scared about Dad. I got him a blackberry which was his favorite and he ate it while we sat on a bench near the stand.

"Are you sure I didn't hurt Marlo's arm?" he asked.

"I'm sure, Rooster," I said. "She was just trying to get a lot of attention from B.J. and that lifeguard. Her arm is fine."

"Dad's going to spank me," he said and his lip was trembling again. "I bet that dumb B.J. will come over and tell Dad everything that happened. And he'll believe him cause he thinks he's such a nice boy."

"Oh, Rooster. I don't think B.J. would come over just to tell on you. If he does, I'll tell Dad the things Marlo was saying."

"How come B.J. didn't help you, Staci? How come he just let that lifeguard kick Rooster out of the pool and didn't say anything about Marlo being so nasty?" Beth was sipping the flavored juice out of her snow cone, looking at me suspiciously.

I had to admit I wasn't pleased that B.J. hadn't said anything in our defense. But he probably hadn't heard Marlo talking to the other girls. He might not have even believed it had Rooster told him.

"Well, that was a quick swim," my father said when we came through the door. "But it's a good thing you came back. That cat of Grandpa's is acting sick again. Maybe you can make her feel better."

Rooster and Beth ran toward the den. I thought about my telescope sitting in the attic and how badly I wanted to go up there and work on it. But I felt I should check on the cat first.

I hung our towels in the bathroom and then went to the den. Harvey was lying on an old blanket beside the fireplace and her sides were heaving just the way they'd been the night before. I wondered if Andy were home and decided I could just do the same things he had done last night. I carried her carefully to the kitchen and made her drink from a bowl of water. I stroked her back as she drank, marveling at how huge her sides were getting, how really enormous she was growing. "How many kittens do you guys think she'll have?" I asked the kids.

"I think four," Beth said.

Rooster rolled his eyes. "I think twelve. Maybe more."

"That's quite a few, Rooster. I don't know as I've ever heard of a cat having twelve kittens." I looked at her again. "I think she'll have five or six."

Harvey lapped at the water until she'd had enough. "Okay," I said. "Let's take her outside and see if it will help as much as it did last night."

"Why don't we get Andy?" Rooster asked. "I think she felt better because he was petting her. Harvey likes Andy better than us 'cause she's known him longer."

"Maybe," I said. "But I hate to bother him again. Let's just see if we can take care of her ourselves."

We carried her outside and the kids went right to their swing set. I sat in the thick grass and held the cat on my lap, stroking her and wondering how long before the kittens would finally be born.

I was still holding Harvey when I heard a tremendous rustling in the hedgerow and a big yell. Then I heard Rooster and Beth laughing like crazy. When I turned toward the hedge, I saw Andy lying in a heap. He was starting to sit up and he was laughing, too, as he brushed grass off his arms and legs and wiped at a scratch.

"What happened to you?" I hollered.

He got up and walked toward me, looking

embarrassed. There was a silly grin on his face. "I jumped the hedge and my shoelace got caught. I fell," he said sheepishly.

"Graceful, Andy." I smiled. "Real graceful."

He sat down beside me and pulled Harvey onto his lap. "Is she sick again?"

"Yeah. She's acting just like she did last night." I looked at him. "Do you think she's going to be all right? I mean, I thought cats just did this with no problem. If anything happens to her, Andy, those kids will never get over it."

"I understand," he said. He kept stroking Harvey and looking at her carefully. "I don't know. She seems fine except for getting nauseated all the time. I'm sure she'll be okay, Staci."

"What if I took her to a vet?"

"That might not be a bad idea. We could take her to Dr. Stanton, down by the Safeway. That's where we take our dog."

"Wait here," I said, jumping up. "I'll go ask Dad, and if he doesn't care we'll take her now."

I hurried into the house and found my father sitting in the den working on a stack of papers. "Dad," I said. "I think Harvey is really sick. Would it be all right if Andy and I took her to that vet down by the store? He could tell us what's wrong."

My father looked up and sighed. "Staci, it

will cost at least twenty dollars to take her in, even if he's open, which he probably isn't. She's just having kittens and I'm sure she'll be fine once they're born."

"But, Dad. She doesn't act right. I want a doctor to look at her and say what's wrong." I was staring at him and I could hear the whining, begging sound in my voice. "I'm scared that something might happen to her and Rooster and Beth won't be able to stand it if she dies."

My father gave me a hard look and I could tell I'd upset him. "They've gone through worse, Staci. I doubt if that cat . . ." He stopped, putting his hand to his forehead and groaning. "Just forget it. If the cat isn't better by Monday, we'll discuss it again. But for now, not another word."

He shuffled his papers around and cleared his throat. I knew he was dismissing me. I turned and went slowly back outside where I found Harvey sprawled on Andy's lap looking perfectly fine and purring her head off. The kids sat at Andy's feet and he was telling them a story about an old hobo camp that used to be located down by the tracks, about three blocks from our house. Rooster and Beth were enraptured by the story even though I could tell Andy was making about half of it up.

When he looked at me, I shook my head. He raised his eyebrows as if asking why my father would say no and I just shrugged. "Okay, you kids," Andy said. "This crazy feline seems a lot better so why don't you take her in the house and put her on her blanket in the den?" He placed Harvey in Beth's arms very gently and the kids went inside.

"What's the deal?" Andy asked after they left.

"He says she's just pregnant and she'll be fine after the kittens." I bent my head so Andy wouldn't see the tears which rimmed my eyes. I wasn't sure if I was crying about Harvey or about the fact that my father and I had failed to communicate again.

Andy was sitting in the grass watching me closely. "Is that all he said, Staci? You seem awfully upset."

I felt my eyes sting again. "It's just about all, Andy. The thing that upsets me is all the stuff my father won't say, all the things he pretends."

"Like what?"

I just shook my head. "It's too hard to explain. You'd have to live with him all the time to understand what I'm talking about."

Andy put his hand on my chin and lifted my face so I was looking straight into his eyes. They were green and my mind whirled with silly, disconnected thoughts. Why hadn't I ever noticed Andy Warren's eyes before? I'd always seen his braces, never looked beyond his silly grin and those games he played with

Rooster. But he was nice, really nice, and I felt bad about all the times I'd sent him home, telling him I was just too busy to talk.

We sat there for another twenty minutes, saying nothing. Andy seemed to understand that I didn't feel like talking. I was comfortable with him, glad to have him sitting with me. I'd probably felt that way a hundred times over the past twelve years.

But I couldn't explain to Andy what was going on inside me right now, how my family was slowly falling apart in subtle ways. I mean, I knew we looked like we were doing all right on the surface—but underneath there were so many things that were just . . . not right.

I lay back in the grass and closed my eyes, wanting to forget about everything. In my mind I could still feel B.J.'s kiss from the night before when we'd gotten home from our date. Why, I wondered, had B.J. told Marlo all about taking me out? And why had he told her I was lonely? Lonely? Sure, I was, sometimes. But wasn't everyone?

I opened my eyes and gazed at Andy. "Are you ever lonely?" I asked.

He smiled. "Sure. Sometimes, when I go to my room at night, I feel lonesome. But I hate to sit around in the den all the time and watch TV with my family. It's confusing, isn't it?"

"Yeah. There have been times when I was the most alone sitting at the dinner table with

Dad, Beth, and Rooster. But that's normal for people our age, isn't it?"

"I hope so," Andy laughed. "We've both got enough strikes against us without having something else that's abnormal."

"Have you thought any more about being a veterinarian when you grow up?"

"Uh huh. I even mentioned it to my father. He got so excited you wouldn't believe it."

"Don't let that change your mind," I grinned.

"Naw, I won't. I really think you've hit on something that I can see myself doing for the next fifty years. Before, when I thought about a career, I just couldn't imagine sticking with it for my whole life." His eyes sparkled and I was struck again by their lovely shade of green. "There are so many rewarding things about being a vet. I mean, I love animals and I might even like to do research on their diseases and try to help them in other ways."

I felt myself smiling. "We've still got two years to make up our minds, you know. I'm still pretty sure I want to go into the astronaut program but every once in a while I wonder if I'll have enough patience to weather the waiting period to find out if I've been accepted."

"You will be," Andy said. "You have a lot to offer NASA. And I can't think of a single person who is more patient when it comes to waiting for something you really want."

Andy stood up. "Call me if Harvey gets sick again," he said. "I wouldn't be too surprised if she has those kittens in the next couple of days."

"I hope so," I said.

He waved and started across the yard.

"Thanks, Andy," I called after him. "Thanks for everything."

6

"Look at Harvey eat," Rooster cried Monday morning after I'd set her bowl down on the floor.

"You're right." I smiled. She was eating much more and there was no doubt in my mind that she was feeling a whole lot better. Yesterday, and again this morning, she had been active and enthusiastic about her food and water. When Beth, Rooster, or I held her, she purred and rolled over to have her throat stroked.

I was glad. This was a big day for me and I wanted everything to go just right. I had planned my day carefully so I'd have lots of time to work on my telescope and still start getting ready for the astronomy meeting by four-thirty. Yesterday I'd worked for more than six hours and I was starting to see results as the mirror took on more and more of a concave appearance. I'd finished the first two grinding steps and, following the instructions that came with the kit, I'd checked the mirror for the first time last night.

This was done with a tin can which had a light bulb inside. I punched a tiny hole in the can, turned off all the lights in the attic, and trained the little beam of light on the mirror. I was pretty sure everything was progressing nicely but I was anxious to have my work double-checked by one of the other people in the club soon. Preferably B.J.

When I thought about having him check it, having him up in the attic with all the lights out, my heart thumped the way it had the night he'd kissed me. B.J. would be very proud when he saw how far I'd gotten on the project. I could imagine him apologizing and telling me how he'd misjudged me, how I was the first girl he'd met who took her science interests seriously. Something about that imagined conversation bugged me a little. Why did B.J. have such a rotten opinion of girls? Andy didn't.

But I decided B.J. just hadn't met any girls with long-range goals and strong motivation before. After a while, he'd realize there were lots of girls who were capable of accomplishing a great deal in life.

I finished feeding Rooster and Beth their breakfast and I even talked them into helping straighten up the kitchen. By now they were getting used to hurrying up to the attic as soon as we had eaten and they didn't give me any trouble as I herded them toward the stairs.

We were just starting up when the doorbell rang. I hurried to answer it and saw Andy standing on the porch.

"What're you doing?" he asked when I opened the door.

I smiled weakly. "Trying to get upstairs to work. Want to come up and talk?" I asked, hoping he'd say no.

"Sure. How's Harvey this morning?"

"She's fine," I said. "Much better."

"Come see," Rooster said in a voice that would have carried all the way across Puget Sound. "She ate all her breakfast."

"Which is more than I can say for you, Rooster," I muttered. "You go check on the cat, Andy. I'm going on up and I'll see you in a few minutes."

Beth stayed with Andy and Rooster and I had gotten a good start by the time they all came upstairs. My hands were covered with the moist, gritty sand and Andy laughed when he saw me working. "Still the same determined Staci," he said. "You know if you gave yourself an hourly salary for that work, you could buy three or four telescopes for what you'll have invested in that one."

"Maybe," I said. "But you can't put a price on the good feeling you get when you do something that's really a challenge. You should try it sometime."

"I'd love to. But it might be difficult. You see, I've got this crazy neighbor who comes and gets me at odd hours, even in the middle of the night, to check on her cat."

I laughed. "Okay, you made your point. Sorry, Andy."

"No problem. How's the telescope coming?"

"Good. It really is. I checked the curvature last night for the first time and I'm really getting excited."

"Listen, Staci. I came over this morning to make you a deal. I'm going to the zoo and I thought I'd take Rooster and Beth off your hands for awhile so you could get more work done."

"That's great, Andy," I said. "But you don't have to do that."

"I want to. There's just one catch to the deal. There's a special show at the museum Wednesday night with laser light beams. If I take the kids today, you have to promise to go to the museum with me next Wednesday night. Is that a deal?"

I grinned at him. "Sure. But I'm getting the better end of the deal. Are you sure you can handle these heathens?"

"Of course. They never give me any trouble."

"I've noticed," I said, laughing. "They save the really big stuff for me."

I wiped my hands on a towel and started toward the stairs. "You kids go wash up and, Beth, bring me the hairbrush."

They hurried down, excited about their trip to the zoo.

"This is really nice of you, Andy."

"Ahh," he leered. "I'll get even when I take you to the museum. I may make you sit through the show twice."

I giggled at his purposeful expression and went down to brush Beth's hair. This was a blessing I hadn't expected. With the kids gone, I could work for almost six uninterrupted hours before I had to get ready to go to Mercer Island.

When they got ready to leave, I tried to give Andy a couple dollars for a treat for the kids but he wouldn't take it. "I've got a little money. You can save that for another time."

Rooster and Beth were jumping up and down. I had to remind them twice to behave themselves and not get wild while they were at the park. "And don't eat a bunch of junk," I said. "You know how Dad hates that."

After they left I poured a great big glass of tea and hurried upstairs. The day passed quickly and I got all kinds of work done before I had to quit and go down to take a bath.

It was nearly five when Andy and the kids came back. By then I was dressed and had my hair in rollers. I was down in the kitchen making beef patties and cutting up some pickles and onions for hamburgers. I had ice tea and cottage cheese on the table. This was about as informal as Dad ever let me get with dinner and I had already discussed it with him at breakfast. I was getting really excited about tonight's meeting.

The kids came bounding into the room, jumping around and telling me about their trip to the zoo. I could tell they'd had a good time. Both of them had dirty faces. Their hands and faces were covered with cotton candy and chocolate. Andy was walking behind them and he looked exhausted. I started laughing.

"Not as easy as you thought, huh?"

He groaned dramatically and sank into a chair. "Help. Have you got a glass of Coke or anything cold for a slave who has just been dragged through the ape house and the elephant pen twelve times?"

I poured him a glass of tea. "You're a good sport, Andy. I hope they didn't run you too hard."

"You have no idea, Staci. Why didn't you tell me these two were monkey freaks?"

"I didn't know." I laughed. "We've only been to the zoo once and that was three years ago with Grandpa."

"You're kidding," Andy gasped. "You, Staci Callahan, haven't been to the zoo in three years?"

"Right. Am I missing something relevant to my social development?"

"Are you ever! I insist that we go again before the summer is over and that you go with us. Darwin would be appalled if you didn't even investigate his theory in person."

"Andy. How can I?" I was scrubbing the telltale evidence of all the sugary treats off Rooster and Beth so my father wouldn't have a fit. They were supposed to be limited to two such gooey things a day but I figured there were times when the rule should be waived. "Just how am I supposed to finish my telescope if I go running off to the zoo?"

"All work and no play makes Staci turn into a frog," Andy said.

Rooster giggled. "You've got it all mixed up, Andy. Princes get turned into frogs."

"Oh, yeah?" Andy said, making his eyes go all wide and wild looking. "Have you ever seen a girl who forgets to have fun? She gets green bulging eyes and warts. Then she starts leaping around rooms all day going, *ribbet, ribbet.*" He was hopping around the kitchen doing a very good imitation of a frog when my father walked in.

"What's going on here?" he asked.

"Hello, sir," Andy said, straightening up quickly and laughing. "I was just trying to talk Staci into going to the zoo with us some day. She never seems interested in anything except work."

"She does seem to get involved. But I guess that won't hurt her. I may not really approve of my daughter wanting to become an astronaut but if she's going to do it, she'll have to learn to work even harder."

"You're right, Mr. Callahan," Andy said. "But maybe before she gets started, she could go to the zoo just once."

"Okay, people," I said. "I have to leave in about forty minutes, so you'd better eat." I set the plate of hamburgers on the table and turned to Andy. "Want to stay for dinner? It isn't fancy but it's ready."

"Are you kidding?" he gasped, holding his stomach and doing a mock faint. "I ate enough junk food at the zoo to keep a hundred rats going in lab tests."

I was shaking my head at him frantically, trying to signal that this might not be a good time to discuss Rooster and Beth's sugar-filled outing. But Andy kept rolling around and Dad was looking at all four of us. "You already went to the zoo?" he asked. "I hope none of you kids have been eating junk food."

"Not me," Rooster said, trying hard to tackle a big hamburger that I knew he didn't want.

"Me either," Beth said.

"Who went to the zoo?" my father asked.

I looked at him and cleared my throat. "Andy offered to take the kids so I could have a free day to work on my telescope."

"That was very kind of him. However . . ." He looked at the kids more closely. "Did you or did you not eat a bunch of junk food?"

"Just a little," Beth said.

"Yeah," Rooster added. "I only ate two hotdogs, two cotton candys, and a carmel apple and one of those chocolate chicken legs."

My father looked stern. "I'm not blaming you, Andrew," he said. "But Staci knows our rules. She broke them when she failed to tell you they were not allowed sweets. I'll have to consider very carefully whether I'm going to allow her to attend that meeting tonight."

"Dad," I wailed. "I didn't think you'd mind if the kids went out for a while, and I just forgot to tell Andy about the sugar." I was staring at Andy, hoping he wouldn't bolt and run out of our house forever once he'd seen how unreasonable my father could be.

"Mr. Callahan," Andy said. "Please don't blame Staci. All the junk I let them eat was my fault. My mom has about the same rules you do, sir, so I should have known better. Please don't take my poor judgment out on Staci."

Dad just shook his head for a moment. I was watching him and feeling really mad. His rules might be all right for every day, but why couldn't he understand that there were times when it was okay to break the rules, days that were too special to wrap up in tight-fitting restrictions? I remembered how excited Rooster and Beth had been when they'd raced in from the zoo and thought how sad it was that Dad was ruining their good feeling.

Both of the kids were looking down at their plates and picking at the food as if they could make everything all right again if they could only manage to gag down a few bites. "Dad, I'm sorry," I said. "I'll watch their diets closely, from now on. Just please let me go to that meeting tonight."

"All right," my father sighed. "I'll overlook it this time, Staci. And, Andrew, I expect you to remember our rules now that you're aware of them." Dad picked up his hamburger and started to eat, apparently ending the discussion.

I walked Andy to the door and thanked him for helping me out all day. "I'm sure sorry about my father," I said in a low voice. "He just seems to be getting worse and worse. He never has any fun anymore and it's getting where he doesn't want us to, either."

"Yeah, I've noticed." Andy patted my shoulder. "Things will get better, Staci. They'll have to. Don't forget, we've got a date for the laser light show on Wednesday night. The hottest show in town." He laughed as he walked down the front steps and I had to smile. Andy's sense of humor wasn't much more advanced than Rooster's but I enjoyed him every once in a while.

I hurried upstairs and started taking my rollers out of my hair. I glanced at the clock while I brushed my hair down over my shoulders. It was already six o'clock. I needed to be at the library in thirty minutes and I was glad I'd dressed before fixing dinner. My jeans were old favorites and I turned so I could see the back of myself in the mirror. A nice tight fit but not too tight, not enough to make my father complain. I was wearing a blue tube top with a white shirt over it. All in all, I decided I looked pretty decent.

I applied a little powder and blush and a light shade of lipstick. Looking in the mirror, I hesitated. Then, without giving myself time to really think about it, I carefully brushed a faint stroke of blue eye shadow over each eye. I leaned back and cocked my head, trying to catch a quick glance of myself as others might see me. The effect was a surprise. I looked . . . well, almost pretty. I knew my father wouldn't like it. I wasn't sure I even liked it myself but still, I was surprised how my eyes stood out more and my whole face looked older.

I ran down the stairs and shouted a farewell to my family. "Sorry, Dad. But I'm late and I've got to run. I'm riding home with B.J. so I won't have to call you for a ride."

"Eleven, Staci," Dad hollered. "At the latest."

"Okay. Bye, kids. Take care of Harvey." I heard them yell good-bye as I raced out the front door.

Andy was standing in his front yard and I

almost stopped when I saw him. "Bye, Andy," I said, hurrying past him. "I'm late for my meeting."

"Bye, Staci," he called.

The blocks between my house and the library seemed extra long as I ran. Stan Franke and several of the other guys were standing in front of the building and there were three cars parked at the curb. "Hurry, Staci," Stan called. "We're getting ready to leave."

I ran up to them, smiling and relieved that I'd made it. All I could think about now was the wonderful evening that was before us, an evening which would include spending several hours with B.J. The fact that Marlo would also be there seemed to dampen my spirits very little. "Thanks for waiting, you guys," I said, breathing heavily and leaning against a pale blue Ford.

"You're welcome," Doug Wilson said. He winked at Stan. "Shall we tell her we were waiting for Jim and Tony or let her think we waited just for her?"

"Oh, by all means, just for her." Stan grinned. "Want to ride with me, Staci? So far there's no one in my car except Doug."

"Sure." I smiled. "I'm really anxious to get out to the island and take part in an honest to goodness observation session."

"Then jump in the Camaro over there. I can see Jim and Tony coming now and they're riding with Fred anyway."

We all hurried over to a yellow Camaro and

I got in the front with Stan. Doug got in the back. The windows were down as we started out and I felt a surge of excitement as my hair whipped in the wind and the salty aroma of Puget Sound filled the air.

"How long will it take us to get over to the island?" I asked.

"Depends on the traffic." Stan was yelling at me. There was no way to communicate in the whipping wind without yelling. But it was fun, exhilarating in a way that was marvelous. I felt like those kids always looked in movies, racing off to the beach in a convertible with the top down. This was exactly the kind of thing that my father would disapprove of, not that we were doing anything wrong, it was just the image we might present to people passing in other cars. I grinned, feeling the pressure of the wind against my face as Stan drove onto the freeway.

Everything felt so unbridled and free as we rushed down Interstate 5. I thought about the kids in the movies again. I never saw them have to go ask their parents if they could go to the beach. Movie teenagers seemed to have all the freedom in the world. I smiled. Usually, in the end, just to show such behavior wasn't always a good idea, the director would have one kid get injured or maybe killed. I decided that was supposed to show the rest of us, dull kids like me stuck in places like Seattle, that nothing bad would ever happen to us if we always remembered to get permission from our parents before going out.

The fact that I knew my father would be furious if he saw me right now made the ride more exciting. Tom Callahan's oldest daughter was off on her own for the night, racing down the freeway in a yellow Camaro and laughing her head off as the wind whipped her hair all over, even out the window. Tom Callahan's oldest daughter might even pig out on sweets and sugary goodies. I laughed out loud. "I love your car, Stan. It's really something."

"I'm glad, Staci," Stan yelled back. "Maybe we can go for a ride alone sometime." He grinned at Doug in the back.

Before long we got off the freeway and headed down Ranier Avenue which would lead us to the long bridge over to the island. Traffic got quite heavy at this point and we had to go pretty slow. I kept glancing at people in other cars, trying to look cool and sophisticated.

"Are you anxious for it to get dark?" Doug asked.

I nodded. "I'm supposed to be home by eleven so I won't have a lot of time. What time are you going back?"

"About then," Stan said. "I have to be up at six to go to work so I wasn't planning to stay too late. I hope you didn't eat. B.J. called this afternoon and said they were going to have a fire going when we arrived. Marlo's dad bought enough hot dogs, buns, and marsh-mallows for the whole club."

Must be nice to have a father like that, I thought. Mine would have his face down, peering in everyone's mouth to make sure they weren't eating a bunch of cavity-causing treats. "I didn't eat. I was running late and didn't have time."

"We've got to go clear around to the south-east side of the island," Stan said. "There's an open beach there that's perfect for the tele-scopes and it also has a great view of Mount Ranier. Usually we look at the mountain until it's dark."

"That's terrific." I smiled. "When I finish my telescope maybe we can come out here again."

"Oh, we do this five or six times a year," Doug said. "Once in a while we come out on a Friday or Saturday night and then we stay a lot later. There was one weekend when just the guys came out and we camped on the beach for two days."

That sounded like fun; more scenes from the beach bikini movies ran through my mind. I could imagine my father if I told him I wanted to camp on the beach at Mercer Island for a couple days with a bunch of boys. Marlo's dad would send food. Mine would send a firing squad.

Stan pulled off the road into a wide parking

area covered with gravel. There were already three cars there including Marlo's red Trans-Am. We got out of the car and Doug pointed to a rocky bank. "We have to climb down those rocks," he said. "I'm sure B.J. found some way to drive along the shore this morning with the telescopes but the tide is coming in and we can't risk taking our cars down now."

I jumped up on one of the rocks and peered over the edge. Below, I could see a high-flaming fire built with huge chunks of drift-wood. At least seven club members were down on the beach picking up more wood or fiddling with telescopes. Marlo was wearing a bright pink bikini. I could see her clearly and it almost made me decide not to go down. Everytime I thought I looked pretty much all right, Marlo showed up looking at least five hundred times better.

Give up, I thought. You'll never be able to compete with her. She's got everything, in-cluding B.J. I could see him down on the beach, chasing Marlo across the sand and rocks. Both of them were wearing tennis shoes because the stones here could cut feet badly.

Stan, Doug, and I started climbing down the rocky face of the cliff and I felt exhilarated as the wind tossed my hair around my face and the smell of fresh water filled the air. Gulls screamed over our heads and I wanted to jump around reveling in the sheer joy of my few hours of freedom. The others had seen us coming now and they were waving us down to the beach. Back up on the road I could hear the slamming of car doors and knew that more club members had arrived.

Doug and Stan helped me over a couple of places where the rocks were especially steep and hard to maneuver around. Soon we were at the bottom of the cliff and hurrying across the stony beach toward the others.

"Glad you made it," B.J. said, smiling.

"Me too." I grinned. "This is really great."

"Didn't you bring a swimming suit?" Marlo asked and I could see that familiar sneer of hers starting to form.

"Yes, I did. It's in my bag but I didn't know the schedule out here so I just wore my jeans."

"Well, run and get into your suit," B.J. said. "There's a private little cove over there behind those rocks. You can change there."

I hurried to the spot he'd indicated. Everything out here was terrific, too terrific to let Marlo wreck it for me. I changed quickly and ran back to the others, throwing my rolled-up jeans and shirt in a pile by all the towels. The sun was lowering now since it was almost seven-thirty but it still sent warm rays across the beach which warmed my back and shoulders. I went and stood near the fire where Stan and Doug were talking to B.J.

"You ready for a big meal?" B.J. asked.

"I could eat a cow." I smiled. "How long before we'll be able to start observing?"

"Right now, if you like. Most of the telescopes are aimed at Mount Ranier at the moment. Go look. I think you'll be surprised how much you can see."

I trotted over to the group of telescopes. Marlo's stuck out like a chrome toothpick. I ignored her instrument and went to one of the others. The rest of them looked pretty much the same, the way I hoped mine would look when I'd finished all the work. They had a homemade appearance that gave testimony to the many long hours of work that had gone into them.

I put my eye to the lens and gasped. The telescope was trained on Mount Ranier as B.J. had said but I couldn't believe how close the mountain appeared. I could actually make out the trees and see snowy places clearly. I didn't know what I'd expected. Anything that could reveal the rings around Saturn would have to be very powerful. Still, the close image amazed me.

"This is incredible," I gasped when Doug walked up and began looking through another telescope.

"Yeah, I know. The first time I did this, I was just as amazed as you are."

"Okay," B.J. hollered. "The fire is ready. If you want to eat you'd better get over here. We've got another hour before we'll be able to

start observing but let's go ahead and pig out
so we can talk for a while and get everything
cleaned up before dark."

I looked at Doug and he grinned. "B.J.'s a
bit of a drill sergeant on these outings," he
said. "But you'll get used to it and he always
manages to make sure we have plenty of time
with the telescopes which is the real reason
for coming out here."

"Oh, I understand," I said. I was staring at
B.J. as Doug and I hurried across the beach.
He was standing quite close to the fire and I
was struck again by his rugged good looks. He
was wearing rust colored bathing trunks that
seemed to bring out the auburn tints in his
hair. He had a deep tan and somehow he
resembled a bronze god holding court for his
subjects from his place beside the roaring
campfire.

All the club members converged on the
hotdogs and sticks which were stacked near
the towels. Everyone found a rock or a place
on the sand and sat down to roast a weiner. I
noticed Marlo didn't move more than three
feet away from B.J. as we all found places.
Then she turned to him and asked him to go
get her hotdog. "Please, B.J.," she said in a
sickeningly sweet voice. "I'll hold our spot."

Like a robot, B.J. trotted to do her bidding
and I wondered if he ever told her "no."
Probably not, I decided. Marlo was the kind of
girl who would have her husband fetching
and heeling by the time she'd been married a

week. And the poor slob would do it for the rest of his life just to have the pleasure of being at her side.

Soon we were all seated around the fire, cooking and eating one hotdog after another. Something about the fresh air, the pounding waves of Lake Washington and the wonderful smell of the great outdoors must have affected all our appetites. We ate as though we were all starved. The food tasted a hundred times better than it would have indoors.

"I want to thank Marlo and her dad for providing all the food," B.J. said. "I think it was a terrific thing for them to do." We all nodded and thanked Marlo.

"Well, Staci," Marlo said. "I imagine you're pretty excited about this trip. Here you just went out on your first date the other evening and now you're out on the beach with all these guys."

"Cool it, Marlo," Stan said. Several other guys murmured agreement.

"What did I do?" Marlo pouted.

I didn't hear much more of the conversation. I got up, threw my paper plate in the fire, and stomped back across the beach to look at Mount Ranier through one of the telescopes. I hated Marlo for trying to embarrass me in front of the entire astronomy club. Just because B.J. had told her he'd taken me on my first date, she felt she had to tell everyone else.

The sun was going down and I knew it

would soon be time to train the telescopes on Venus and begin the observation session. I was shivering and decided to go slip into my jeans and my shirt before we started. Most of the mess had been cleaned up when I walked back. The fire was dying down and there was an air of tranquility on the beach that was unlike anything I'd ever experienced. If it hadn't been for the tension between Marlo and myself, I would have been totally content.

I was just zipping my jeans when she walked over and put her hand on my shoulder. "Staci, I didn't mean to hurt your feelings. I don't know what gets into me sometimes. I'm the kind of person who always says what I'm thinking and I never stop to think that others might take it wrong. Will you forgive me?"

I looked at her, trying to decide if I could trust her or if this was just another trick to get me off balance. She slid a T-shirt over her bikini while I watched her. She seemed sincere enough and her eyes, when she gazed at me, were warm for the first time.

"Sure, Marlo," I finally mumbled. "I'll forgive you. But only if you stop trying to embarrass me in front of all these guys."

"I promise, Staci. I'll be able to help you a lot around school next fall. You'll see. I know just about everybody."

I smiled and she hugged me quickly and then we hurried toward the guys who were all standing around the telescopes making the necessary adjustments as they trained them on Venus which was already visible in the darkening sky.

We observed the planet for over an hour, each of us getting several turns at one of the scopes as B.J. asked questions and took notes. I felt timid at first about making positive statements about things I saw but pretty soon I was talking and taking part as much as anyone else.

I was having one of the best times in my life. I felt so much a part of this group that for the first time I was actually glad that we had moved to Seattle. Marlo made an effort several times to talk to me, to include me in conversations as the session continued. Twice she asked me to look through her telescope and I had to admit it was the most powerful one in the club. As the evening progressed, I felt bad that I'd judged her so harshly.

She smiled at me when I finished looking through her telescope. "I think it's almost time to go, Staci. I hope you make it to the meeting next week. And remember, I want to help you meet people and make friends when school starts."

"That's really nice of you," I said.

"Oh, I want to," she said. "Call me some afternoon and we'll go shopping together. I know exactly what everyone's getting for school and I can make sure you buy just the right things."

I looked down, knowing there was very little money for school clothes this year. What there was would be spent mostly on Beth and Rooster since they grew faster and most of their stuff didn't fit them anymore. Then I remembered the money I had put in the bank for college. My father wouldn't have to know if I took some of it out to buy clothes.

"That's a great idea, Marlo," I said. "I hate to shop alone. I'll call you a little closer to time for school to start. And thanks a lot for the offer."

"I need some help loading these telescopes," B.J. said. "I think this has been one of our best sessions ever."

We all smiled and nodded agreement. For me it was the best, better than I had ever dreamed it could be. And Marlo and I were friends now. At least we were on the way to becoming friends and once she knew me better, after we'd been shopping and all, I felt sure we'd become close friends.

I helped Stan put sand on the remainders of the campfire as the telescopes were pulled carefully up the cliff. B.J. and the others had to walk about two hundred yards down the beach to find a place where they could even get them up the steep hill.

Soon we were all standing around in the parking lot saying our good-byes. I hated the evening to end. But it was getting late and I'd have a hard time with my dad if we got home after eleven.

B.J. pulled me aside just as I was getting ready to get in Stan's car. "Hey, Staci," he said. "I've been trying to find a chance to talk to you all evening."

I looked at him, not remembering a time when I'd been too busy to talk. "What do you need, B.J.?"

"I want to take you to a movie Wednesday night. No more putt-putt, lady. I learned my lesson the other night. You're the champ at that and I concede. So, will you go to a movie?"

My heart was fluttering. I'd accepted the fact that he'd never ask me out again and this was really a surprise. Then I remembered my promise to go to the museum with Andy Wednesday night. I felt sick. How could I get out of the date with Andy without hurting his feelings? Still, Andy should want me to have a good time and I was sure he knew how I felt about B.J.

"Staci?" B.J. said. "Do you want to go to the movies Wednesday?"

I smiled at him but I was feeling awful on the inside. "Sure, B.J., I'd love to go with you. Just call and let me know what time."

Marlo walked up just then. She smiled thinly as she took hold of B.J.'s arm. There was something about her eyes, though, that made me feel uncomfortable. They seemed to glint like black rocks in the moonlight, looking strange and out of place with the smile.

I climbed into Stan's car for the ride home, thinking how I should feel really good about everything. But I didn't. Wednesday night kept flashing through my mind and I wondered if Andy'd be as understanding as I'd thought about me breaking our date.

And Marlo's cold eyes. Was she angry again? Surely not. Everything was going to be fine, I decided, as I leaned back and enjoyed the ride. It was only ten-twenty. We'd make it home just in time.

7

The next morning I woke up thirty minutes before my alarm clock went off. I had this horrendous feeling of guilt as I lay there wondering if I'd be able to explain to Andy why I was breaking our date. I tossed around for several minutes and then jumped up, turned off my alarm, and made the bed.

The best thing to do was get busy, start doing my chores so I could get up to the attic and work on my telescope. If I worked hard enough, maybe I could get rid of the rotten feelings inside me.

I thought about Andy as I hurried downstairs to fix breakfast. Why couldn't he have left our relationship the way it had been for years? Now that he'd asked me out, everything had changed. I was on this guilt trip instead of basking in the joy of going out with B.J. again.

I slammed pots and pans around, trying to get myself under control. Dad walked into the kitchen and gave me a funny look as he sat down at the table. He didn't say anything though and I was grateful. Something about what I'd done to Andy was so distasteful I knew I wouldn't want my father to know.

I fried two eggs for him, keeping my back turned so he couldn't see my guilty expression.

It seemed to take my father forever to leave the house and I had to force myself to act normal. All I really wanted was to get upstairs and grind my anxiety away, along with the glass surface of the mirror. By the time Rooster and Beth had come down and eaten breakfast, I was almost frantic to get to the attic.

"What's the matter, Staci?" Beth asked. "Didn't you have any fun at your meeting?"

"Yes," I sighed. "I had a lot of fun. Maybe too much."

"Did you kiss that icky B.J.?" Rooster said, making a weird face.

"No," I snapped. "Now hurry up and help me clean the kitchen so we can go upstairs."

"Do we have to do that again today?" Beth was groaning and flopping around in her chair as if I'd asked her to accompany me into a snake pit.

"Yes, we do. You guys always make me lose

an hour or more of work every day just by stalling. Why can't you cooperate and help me out in the mornings instead of throwing these baby fits?"

Now I'd done it. They were both glaring at me and I knew I'd have to beg at least fifteen minutes and probably bribe them, too, if I hoped to get any work done on the telescope.

Harvey waddled through the kitchen right then and I remembered with a sickening thud that I'd forgotten to feed her. She was standing by the cupboard where we kept her cat-food, meowing pitifully. I braced myself for the accusations of "cat-killer" that I knew were coming.

Rooster and Beth advanced on me. Beth lifted the bulky cat in her arms. "You didn't feed her again, Staci," she said. "All her babies are probably starved inside her and I bet you're glad!"

Rooster didn't even bother to speak. He just opened the cupboard, got a can of food and opened it quickly. They turned their backs on me and walked to Harvey's corner where they set her food down and talked lovingly to her as she ate.

I banged cups and plates around, loading the dishwasher with a vengeance. That stupid cat was getting on my nerves. If she weren't getting sick, she was causing trouble. I could see her pudgy body between the slender figures of Rooster and Beth. My stomach burned painfully and I wished Andy would come over, look at Harvey and assure me she was all right.

But then I remembered what I'd done the night before, how I'd betrayed Andy for a movie with B.J. My stomach hurt even worse. There was no way I could tell him what I'd done without hurting his feelings, maybe even destroy the friendship we'd shared for so many years. I wanted to see him desperately but I was afraid, afraid to let him know what a shallow person I'd become.

Part of me wanted to call B.J. and tell him I'd forgotten a previous commitment when I accepted his invitation. But another part of me refused. I had a right to go out with anyone I wanted. And I wanted to go to a movie with B.J. If Andy was really my friend, he would understand.

"Come on, kids," I said. "Let's straighten the living room and make your beds."

"Why should we?" Beth snarled. "You're being a big grouch this morning and you probably forgot to feed Harvey on purpose."

"I did not forget on purpose, Beth," I objected. "I don't know how Dad expects me to take care of everything around here. He never makes you two do anything." I slammed the dishwasher and started it, listening as water poured into the machine with a force equal to the rage which rushed through my body. B.J. was right. My father was making a slave out of me, making me miss out on all the fun with my friends. I was losing the excitement of being a teenager.

By the time Dad no longer required my services, I would be thirty years old, an old maid with no hope for a future of my own. Rooster and Beth, in the meantime, would continue merrily along with no responsibilities whatsoever.

There was a knock on the back door and my heart skipped about three beats. What if it were Andy?

I took a deep breath and pulled the door open.

Mona Warren, Andy's mother, stood on the porch holding a gigantic bowl of something and smiling a big friendly smile.

"Hello, Mrs. Warren," I stammered, wondering if she had heard my outburst at Beth as she'd walked to the house.

"Hello, Staci," she said, still smiling like crazy. "I baked you a casserole this morning and thought I'd bring it over myself so I could see how you were making out with the children."

"Fine," I said. "We're all doing just fine."

She walked in, opened the refrigerator and put the casserole inside. "You know, Staci, I'm more than happy to help you any way I can. There's very little for me to do at home anymore since Andy's practically grown. I hate to think of a sweet girl like you having all this responsibility when I'm right next door to help."

"I don't need any help," I said. "Honest."

"Now, Staci," Mrs. Warren said, smiling that smile that looked so much like Andy's. "Don't tell me you couldn't use another pair of hands. It's a big job caring for two little ones." She looked around at the stained counter tops and the dirty kitchen floor that still showed evidence of one of Rooster's messy attempts to pour milk for Harvey. "Why don't we work together today? Mop the floors and wash windows. No woman can face these heavy chores without wishing she had a bit of help."

"No, really," I said. "I hate to have you do the chores I'm supposed to do. Dad might even get mad." I was thinking about the day Andy had taken the kids to the zoo.

"Nonsense," Mrs. Warren laughed. "If Tom says anything about it I'll wring his neck."

I laughed. So did Beth and Rooster. The idea of watching Andy's mother wring our father's neck amused all three of us. Maybe it wasn't such a bad idea, I decided. The house was long overdue for a good cleaning and I wasn't sure I even knew how to clean it properly.

"All right, Mrs. Warren. If you really don't mind helping, I'd appreciate it."

That was all the encouragement she needed. In minutes she had assembled a bucket, several sponges and an array of cleaning supplies that I hadn't even known we owned. She shooed the kids into the den and they didn't question her authority at all, just marched away like little angels. I made a mental note to ask them later why they never obeyed me like that.

By the time we had finished cleaning the windows sparkled, the floors glowed with a bright waxy polish and the whole house smelled fresh and clean. Both of us flopped down on kitchen chairs and I smiled at Mrs. Warren. "Thank you," I said. "I never could have done a job like this. Dad will be very pleased with the way the house looks."

"Well, if I know anything about men, he has no idea how to teach you to do these things, Staci. Only a woman can clean a house the way it should really be done."

"Would you like a cup of coffee?" I asked, standing up and turning on the flame under the teakettle.

"That sounds marvelous." Mrs. Warren slipped her shoes off and leaned back in her chair. "You know, Staci. You're such a lovely girl I wish I could be of more help to you. I always wanted a daughter."

My hand stopped in midair as I carried her coffee cup. "Please don't say that," I mumbled. "My mom was a wonderful person. I can't ever be anyone else's daughter."

"I know that, honey," Mrs. Warren said, getting up and walking across the room. I backed away but she followed, putting her arms around my shoulders and hugging me really hard. "I just want to be here when you need me, fill in the lonely places. I knew your

mother well, remember? I'd never try to take
her place. She was too special."

Tears were burning my eyes and I knew I
was going to cry if I didn't get out of that
kitchen. But Mrs. Warren's arms were still
wrapped around me and there was no way to
escape. "My mother was very special," I said.
"Too special for me to pretend anyone could
fill her place."

I broke free and turned toward Mrs. Warren.
"Thank you very much for all your help
today," I sobbed. Then I ran from the kitchen,
fled up the stairs and closed myself in my
room, sobbing like a baby.

Andy's mother followed me and tapped softly on the door for several minutes before giving up and going away. I flopped down on my
bed and cried for a long time, cried for the
mother who had left without saying good-bye
and cried because another woman, a very
nice woman, had thought she could fill the
void.

I tried to make my mother's face come into
my mind, tried to picture the way she used to
look when she was laughing or singing to
Rooster in our old rocking chair in the nur-
sery. But her image wouldn't come to me. I
couldn't remember what my mother looked
like and that made me cry all the harder.
What kind of awful daughter would forget her
mother?

I heard my bedroom door open and looked
up. Rooster and Beth were standing there

gazing at me with frightened eyes. "Are you okay?" Beth asked. They were scared, I could tell. There was nothing I could do to help them, no way I could explain why I was crying so hard.

"I'm fine, you guys," I mumbled. "Please go downstairs. I'll be down in a minute."

For once they didn't ask any questions. They just did what I'd asked. I got up, went to the bathroom and splashed cold water on my face. No matter how rotten I felt, I knew I had to pull myself together for the kids. And Dad. He'd be home in a couple of hours and there was no way he'd understand me going to pieces just because Mona Warren had offered to help me with the kids. But it was more than that and I knew it.

When I went downstairs, I found the kids sprawled out in front of the television set. They weren't watching it; they were just lying there with long faces, looking scared. "Hey, you guys," I said, trying to make my voice sound bright. "What's the matter? You gonna get all upset just because I've been acting like a fool?"

They looked up and I could see the relief in their eyes. Rooster jumped up and bounced around the room, acting dumb. But I was so happy to see them feeling better that I didn't care. "Let's check on Harvey," I said. "Then maybe we can walk down and get a snow cone."

"Sure, Staci," Beth said. "We'll do anything you say."

"Knock it off, silly," I said. "If you two started doing whatever I said all the time, I'd die of shock."

We found Harvey lying on Rooster's bed and she seemed fine. I went to my room for snow cone money and then we hurried downstairs. Just as we started out the front door, I remembered the casserole Mrs. Warren had brought over this morning. If I wanted it to be heated when Dad got in we'd have to hurry.

Rooster and Beth didn't seem to mind the rushed trip and they even cooperated when I made them eat the juicy treats as we walked home instead of sitting on the benches the way we usually did.

When we got back, I turned the oven on and popped the casserole inside. It was four o'clock. I still had to make a salad and heat some bread but there was plenty of time for that. I looked around the house, impressed again with the sparkling floors and windows. Andy's mother was really nice and I felt terrible about the scene I'd made.

Rooster and Beth went out to their swing set and I followed them, sitting down in the thick green grass behind the house. I lay back, letting all the things that had happened in the past two days wash over me in a torrent. There was my new friendship, or at least budding friendship, with Marlo. And another date with B.J. But thinking of that reminded me of Andy and the fact that sooner or later I was going to have to tell him I couldn't go to the museum tomorrow night.

I had closed my eyes when I felt someone come up beside me and sit down. I turned my head, opened my eyes and saw Andy. "What do you want?" I asked, turning away quickly, hoping he had missed my guilty expression.

"I want to talk to you. Help you if I can."

"Your family is full of offers to help today," I said.

"Staci, please don't be so hard on my mom. I know she can be kind of overpowering but she means well. All she wants to do is make your job a little easier."

"And take care of Rooster and Beth and slide into the vacant place our mother left behind." I knew I was being horrible but I couldn't seem to stop. "Why doesn't she just take care of you? Isn't that enough?"

He shook his head. "Not for her. She always wanted about ten kids, I think. And she wanted a girl." He reached out and touched my shoulder. "She likes you, Staci. She really does. Mom knows she can't take the place of your real mother but she can't understand why you don't ever call her."

"I have too much to do," I snapped. "I don't have time to waste like some people I know."

"I think you're riding the crest of some giant guilt trip, Staci. Life can be pretty terrific if you'll let the good times happen."

"Oh, sure. Life is a ball when you've got a

mother and a father and all the other little
extras that most kids take for granted. What
do you know about the bad things?"

"I know a little. So does my mom." Andy
was chewing on a blade of grass and looking
at me strangely. "Before I was born my parents had another son, my brother. He would
be about six years older than me. But he died,
Staci. When he was three, he died in a car
accident. Mom was hurt badly and the doctors
didn't think she'd ever have another baby. But
she did. She had me. I think her attitude made
a lot of difference." He threw a handful of
grass into the air. "So don't tell me you've
done all the suffering. I think everybody gets
a little bit in their life."

I stared at him, feeling rotten. "I'm sorry,
Andy. But really, what's the use?"

"But don't you see, you've been feeling so
sorry for yourself that you don't care who you
hurt? You let your new friends take advantage
of Rooster and Beth, and you close out people
like my mother, who only wants to help.
You're not the Staci I used to know."

I was devastated. How dare he! "Well, if I'm
such a horrible person, you can just forget
about the museum tomorrow night!"

He glared at me. "I might as well. I was
down at the pool this afternoon and B.J. made
it a point to let me know that you two have a
date that night. I guess he has a date with the
new Staci."

Tears stung my eyes. I hadn't wanted to hurt Andy this way. "I'm sorry," I said. "I meant to talk to you, to explain, but you came charging over here with this lecture and you never gave me a chance."

"I don't need to give you any chances, Staci. You take them for yourself." He lifted my chin with his finger and gazed into my eyes. "Just don't take too many chances. You're running in fast company right now. A lot of people won't understand being pushed aside just because you want a shot at being popular." He nodded toward Rooster and Beth who were sitting on their swings and watching us silently. "As for me, I'm not family. I quit understanding at the pool this afternoon." He started to walk away and then turned back. "By the way, I'll try to make sure my mother doesn't hassle you anymore."

"Andy!" I cried. He walked away and he didn't look back.

Rooster ran after Andy and I saw the two of them talk for a few minutes before Andy ruffled my brother's hair and jumped across the hedge. Dad came to the back door looking for us and I steered the kids inside, refusing to answer their questions as I put plates on the table and finished dinner.

My father seemed to sense something was wrong but he just watched me. He didn't even ask his usual questions. Rooster and Beth ate their food silently. Nobody said anything when Dad kept on complimenting about how nice the house looked and how well I was handling my responsibilities.

We'd had a lot of uncomfortable meals before but this one was the absolute worst. Dad talked inanely about things like the weather and his job. I picked at my food while the kids shot curious looks at me when Dad wasn't looking. After dinner, my father went to the den and I sent the kids out of the room, refusing to let them help with the cleaning up.

I might be a creep, I thought as I did the dishes, but Andy was worse. What right did he have to come over and try to impose his ideas on me? And he'd tricked me. He knew about the date with B.J. but he hadn't said anything until I'd made a fool of myself by saying I wouldn't go to the museum first.

I slammed the dishwasher closed. I didn't need Andy or his mother. In fact, I didn't need anybody.

8

I went up to the attic after I'd finished the dishes and tried to work on my telescope for a while, but I couldn't concentrate. My mind kept going over and over the things that had happened. Finally I gave up and went downstairs.

Rooster and Beth were watching TV with Dad so I went to the living room and sat down with a book. The doorbell rang and I grumbled as I got up to answer it. If it was Andy, I decided I'd tell him to leave and never come back. He'd walked away from me this afternoon but he'd never get the chance to do that again. I'd never let him get close enough.

I peered through the peep-hole and saw B.J. and Marlo standing on the front porch. "Hi, you guys. What's up?" I said, opening the door wide.

"B.J. wanted to see how you were coming with your telescope," Marlo said. I stepped back to let them in, admiring her white jogging shorts and flowered halter. Marlo's tan got more spectacular every day.

"I haven't done much today. But I'm making good progress. You want a Coke?" I asked, smiling at them as they sat down together on the couch.

"Sounds great," B.J. said.

"I'll be right back." I hurried to the kitchen and poured three glasses of Coke. Rooster came around the corner from the den and wrinkled his nose, making weird faces to tell me he knew who was here. "Cool it," I whispered. "If you do anything to them this time, I swear I'll break your scrawny bones."

"Uh, uh," he said, smiling smugly. "Dad will spank you if you do something like that."

"Well, Dad might not have to know, Rooster. You just stay out of the living room and keep that cat away, too."

"Who said? Did Dad say I had to stay out?"

"He will if I tell him what happened at the pool the other day with Marlo."

My brother just stared at me with his mouth hanging open and his blue eyes wide. "Staci. You wouldn't do that. We never tell Dad stuff like that."

"I will, Rooster. I swear."

"I won't do anything," he said, letting his

eyes go kind of squinty and mean looking. "But I'll never trust you again, Staci. If you tell Dad things like that, you're breaking our rules."

"I don't care, Rooster," I whispered, leaning close so he'd be sure to get the message. "If blackmail is the only way I can get you to treat my friends right, I'll do it."

"If they're your friends I won't hurt them. I won't play tricks either."

"Go play in the den," I whispered.

"I won't hurt them, Staci, but they'll hurt you. They're mean. That Marlo's the meanest girl I ever met."

He left and I picked up the Cokes and hurried to the living room. "I'm sorry," I said. "I thought we were out of Cokes but I found some more." I was smiling so hard I could feel my lips stretching.

"That's quite all right," Marlo said. "We were just chatting." She hooked her arm through B.J.'s and giggled. I felt uncomfortable but by the time I'd set all the Cokes down Marlo had moved back to her side of the couch and everything seemed better.

"I wish I had more work done," I said. "I'd love to show you guys my telescope but there hardly seems much point."

"We'll see it another time," Marlo said. "Have you thought any more about our shopping trip, Staci?"

I nodded, hoping she wouldn't pursue the subject any further. If my father found out I planned to take money out of my savings for clothes, he'd hit the roof. "We can do it later in the summer, can't we?" I asked. "I mean, there's no hurry."

"Of course not. Say, where's that cute little brother of yours? He can be quite a handful but I have to admit he's adorable."

"He's watching TV with Beth and my father in the den. Don't encourage him to come in here," I said, laughing nervously. "We wouldn't want to take any chances on him pulling one of his famous tricks."

B.J. looked at me. "Where's your mother, Staci? I don't think I've ever met her."

I felt my face burn and fumbled with my Coke glass, running my fingers along the side until I'd wiped all the moisture away. "My mother is dead," I mumbled, not looking up at them.

"I'm sorry," B.J. said. "Why didn't you tell us before?"

"Yes," Marlo said, gasping slightly. "That's just awful."

"She died two years ago. We moved here after my grandfather died and I decided it would be easier if I didn't tell everybody, try to explain all the time about not having a mother and all."

"It can be embarrassing," Marlo said and I stared at her.

Suddenly, I saw myself for the first time as Andy must be seeing me. What kind of daughter had I been? I should have told the truth long ago.

Marlo smiled a smug, knowing smile and I wanted to get up and slap that smirk off her face. But before I could do anything, I saw my father standing in the doorway. His face was distorted with rage.

"Come into the kitchen, Staci," he said. "I'd like to speak to you alone."

I followed him meekly, wondering if he'd heard my discussion with Marlo and B.J.

"Who do you think you are, young lady?" he said, keeping his voice low and frightening as he closed the door behind us. "What right do you have telling personal family matters to these young friends of yours, discussing things that are none of their business?"

"Whose business is it, Dad? I mean, whose business is it that my mother is dead?"

"No one's business. You have no right to sit in my house and talk to them about things like that."

I was crying now and I knew I was raising my voice. "But I have every right to talk about my mother in this house. It's grandpa's house and he was her father. He never made me pretend that Mama was still alive. He talked about her with me, told me funny stories about things she did when she was little. I didn't have to pretend with him, Dad, didn't have to play a stupid game that Mama wasn't dead!"

My father slapped me then, and without another word, spun around and stormed into the living room. I stood in frozen horror, listening as he asked Marlo and B.J. to leave. He was polite in his own way, but I knew this was the most humiliating thing that had happened to me yet, far worse than anything Rooster had done.

I listened in shocked silence as the door closed solidly behind them and then I ran up the stairs, clear up to the attic. The grainy sand felt rough to my fingertips as I worked furiously on my telescope, trying to block out any other sound in the house. I worked with a vengeance, feeling the muscles in my neck and shoulders start to ache as I bent over the mirror and pushed the glass grinding surface back and forth.

Twice, Beth came to the bottom of the stairs and called to me, begged me to come down. I ignored her even though I could tell she was crying.

Darkness fell and I switched on the light, barely breaking stride in my work. The house got quiet. I was aware that the TV had been turned off and the silence convinced me my family had gone to bed. I kept working, hating my father more with every stroke across that mirror. He hadn't even come up to talk to me about our fight, hadn't said he was sorry for slapping me even though he'd never done such a thing before.

I felt like my arms were going to fall off but I

kept grinding that mirror, sliding the opposing piece of glass back and forth, like a robot. I must be a robot or something else without a heart. I'd hurt just about everybody I cared for today.

But I hadn't done anything to Dad. All I'd done was tell the truth finally, admitted to B.J. and Marlo that my mother was dead. The stinging slap on my face hadn't hurt nearly as much as the rejection from my father, the final admission that we were never going to talk about Mom, dignify her life by admitting that she'd once been here on earth, laughing, and loving us all very much. I wanted to go out in the street and shout as loud as I could that I'd once had a mother, a pretty, happy mother who had been one of the finest people I'd ever known.

My nose was running from crying so hard. My arms hurt so much I could barely lift them to wipe the tears away. Exhausted, I finally stopped. I stumbled as I walked toward the stairs, shut off the light and went down to wash my hands. But I couldn't go to bed.

I was out in the backyard, flopped down in the soft grass before I finally let myself go, cry loud and hard like I'd wanted to do all day. The sobs racked my body and I cried until there were no tears left, no more secret sad places that hadn't been touched and wept over.

I kept seeing Rooster's face when I'd been so awful in the kitchen. And Andy's face when I shouted at him this afternoon. Even Mrs. Warren, who was so sweet, trying to figure out why I'd run away from her and shut myself in my room. All day long I had been striking out at people I cared about. Was I really doing all that just so I could be friends with Marlo and B.J.? Sobs shook me again. I wasn't that kind of person, had never been selfish or unkind.

A cloud passed over the moon, making the night as dark as my life felt at that moment.

Images flashed in my mind, pictures from Grandpa's photo albums. My grandparents, young and laughing, as they held their first child and then their second. Then I thought of Rooster and Beth, Rooster and Beth as they looked when they were happy, playing with Harvey or swinging way up in the air on their swing set. Rooster and Beth wouldn't be here if Mama hadn't been born, if my grandparents hadn't had enough courage to take a chance on life.

I wouldn't be here either.

Andy was right. Life would go on. I looked over at his house. It was dark as I walked toward the hedge.

My aching arms protested as I climbed the fat oak tree, and I almost gave up a couple of times. But Andy had been right about everything. I couldn't let the night pass without telling him how sorry I was, what a shallow creep I'd become while trying to make new friends.

I finally reached his window and tapped

lightly on the glass. Before I could tap again, Andy appeared and pulled the curtain aside eagerly, as if he'd been expecting me. He pulled the window open and leaned on his elbows, gazing at me with a little smile.

"Is this a social call or is your cat sick?"

I laughed for the first time in hours. "It's a social visit. Do you have a spot of tea?"

"As a matter of fact, I do." He disappeared for a second and returned with two cans of Coke, both of them cold. "Will this do?"

"Have you been waiting for me, Andy?"

He nodded. "I knew you would come around. People like you never let the sun set on their anger, Staci."

"You're impossible," I giggled. "Want to come over to my house and talk or shall we just sit out here in your tree?"

"Your house is fine. Don't drop your Coke going down the tree. I had a hard time sneaking both of them up to my room."

When we got to the ground I put my drink down and pulled Andy to a halt. "I want to apologize," I said. "Before you go one step further I want you to know that I'm admitting I've been a creep and you were right about almost everything."

"Is there a charge for this compliment? I'm always suspicious when it comes to rapid changes of heart. You know, those things they do in the movies where the villain decides to go straight? Never do another rotten thing as long as he lives?"

We were walking toward my back yard and I reached out and grabbed Andy's hand. "I feel better. All the things you said to me today have had time to sink in and I feel like a new person."

He squeezed my hand. "Glad I could help. If I ever start acting obnoxious, promise me you'll return the favor and insult me out of it."

"Don't worry, Andy. I definitely owe you one. Step one foot out of line and I guarantee I'll return the favor."

We sat down on the grass and the light coating of dew felt cool and damp. I told him most of the things that had happened after he left and he patted my arm gently.

"I'm sorry things have been so rough, Staci. But look at it this way. Unless your father wants the silent treatment to go on forever, he's going to have to give in and talk to you kids about your mother, about all the things that have happened in your family since the day your mom died."

"Maybe, Andy. But what if he decides to ignore this, too? Chooses to go on tomorrow as if nothing happened?"

"He might do that. He's not as flexible as you, Staci. He's been keeping all that hurt bottled up inside because he thinks he's pro-tecting you and the kids." Andy lay back in the cool grass.

"But how can I get him to talk? If we go on like this much longer, I'm afraid there will be no turning back, no way to talk about her at all. Rooster and Beth will be hurt the worst. They were so little their memories will get dimmer and dimmer. Pretty soon they won't remember Mom at all."

"You can help them, Staci. Put her picture out where they can see it. Talk to them about her, remind them of the things you used to do as a family." I could see him looking at me, his eyes reflecting the light from the kitchen window. He was more earnest than I'd ever seen him. "Help those kids, Staci. If your dad can't do it then you'll have to fill the void until he's ready."

"I can't put her picture out, Andy. Dad put them all away after she died. I know he packed them in a box but I can't find it."

"Well, try to convince him somehow that remembering her with pictures and warm discussions is better than hiding the pain away as if she never existed."

"You're a good friend, Andy. I wish I could be more like you." I reached for his hand in the dark and squeezed it tightly. "I'll never be able to make up for what I did, accepting a date with B.J. after I'd told you I'd go to the museum. For some dumb reason I thought you knew how hung up I was on B.J. and I told myself you'd want me to go, want me to be happy."

"I do want you to be happy, Staci. And if B.J. Keller is what it takes to put a smile on your face, then go for it. Just remember I warned you about that crowd. Don't get your hopes up, thinking he'll fall for you or anything like that. For B.J., there is only one person. Marlo Cate. She likes him when it's convenient, dumps him when someone new and exciting comes along and then crooks her little finger at him when things slow down again. And he comes running back like a puppy who needs a good scratching behind the ears."

"Is it that bad?" I asked.

"Worse. I'm only giving you the highlights. I've been watching those two for four or five years and the script never changes. Just the seasons and the players."

"That's terrible," I sighed. We both stood up at the same time as if we knew it was getting late and we should be going in. I hugged Andy and he hugged me back.

"Friends again?" I asked.

"Friends. I would never let a little thing like a humongus fight send me packing."

I turned toward my house. "Thanks, Andy. Thanks for being so understanding about all the crummy things I've done lately."

I went into the house feeling good about myself for the first time that day.

9

The next morning after breakfast I offered to take Rooster and Beth to the library. They had been polite but silent all morning and I hoped the walk and the fresh air would cheer them up.

"Go get your books from last week and brush your hair," I said. "You'll have a good time. I promise."

"I don't feel like going," Rooster whined. "I want to play with Andy and you made him mad. He'll probably never come see us again."

"He's not mad anymore, Rooster. He came over last night and we made up."

"Really?" Beth said. Her eyes were wide and blue this morning as if there were a

151

thousand questions running around inside her head. "Did you make up with Dad, too?"

"Uh uh," I muttered. "He didn't say anything this morning. Except good-bye, that is."

"How come Dad got mad at you, Staci?" Rooster was watching me closely, trying to act casual when I could tell he was really worried.

"I said something that upset him. Let's don't talk about that for a while. Okay?"

They nodded and hurried out of the room, returning a few minutes later with their hair brushed neatly and their library books clutched in their arms.

We climbed the long flight of steps outside the library and Rooster ran ahead of us, trying to pull the heavy glass doors open. He had that swaggering look he got sometimes when he was trying to be the "man of the family," taking care of Beth and I while we were away from Dad. Usually I thought it was cute but today I felt sorry for him. I wasn't the only one in our house with too much responsibility. Rooster had this feeling that he had to take care of us that surfaced every once in a while, making him try to act three times his age.

Once inside, he seemed to forget all about it as he ran toward the children's section. Beth carried their books to the librarian and turned them in before following Rooster.

I started for the science fiction. There was a book about new star discoveries that I wanted to read. Just as I rounded the corner by the card files, I ran into Marlo and three other girls.

They were looking at a copy of *National Geographic* and snickering over one of the pictures. Marlo glanced up, saw me and our eyes locked. My heart pounded as I tried to decide what to do.

Neither of us looked away. We just stared at each other for what seemed like five minutes. I decided to apologize.

"Hi, Marlo," I said, stammering a little and looking down at my feet. "I'm awfully sorry about last night, that scene with my dad and all. He gets upset when we talk about Mom."

Marlo appraised me coolly. Her black eyes felt like they were boring holes in my flesh. Slowly she turned toward her friends. "This is Staci Callahan," she said. "You know, the girl I've been telling you about. Her father threw B.J. and me out of their house last night." She tilted her head to one side and her hair, which was long and flowing like black satin, cascaded around her shoulders.

"It wasn't that way, Marlo," I said. "He was upset."

"I'm not surprised, though," Marlo went on. "You should meet her little brother. He threw me in the pool a few days ago and almost broke my arm." As if remembering her tremendous pain, Marlo clutched her arm. Only she grabbed the wrong arm.

"That's not fair, Marlo," I cried. "You know he didn't almost break your arm."

The librarian walked over, looked at me and placed her finger to her lips. "Shhh. I'll have to ask you kids to leave if you can't be a little more quiet," she whispered.

I saw Rooster and Beth standing beside the card files, almost as if they'd sensed the confrontation with Marlo. I shot them a warning look and turned back to the girls. "You're not being fair," I whispered.

"Not fair?" Marlo gasped. "You girls should hear what her sweet little brother, that's him with the bright red hair, did to B.J. He dumped a pail of water, pail and all, on his head. Poor B.J. could have suffered a concussion or something."

"You weren't even there," I gasped. "That water was meant for me. It was just an accident."

"I think your brother is an accident. A freak of nature."

I glared at Marlo, noticing the three girls beside her seemed to be enjoying the scene immensely. "You're a horrible person, Marlo. You're cruel and mean."

"Really?" she said, opening her eyes wide in mock shock. "By the way, Staci. Your father threw us out before B.J. had a chance to tell you why we really dropped by. He won't be taking you to the movies tonight. Or any other night for that matter. You see, B.J. and I are going steady." She lifted her left hand and pointed to a large class ring with a big wad of adhesive tape holding it in place on her finger.

"He came over to my house to break our date and brought you along?"

"I insisted. You see, Staci, B.J. has the bad habit of feeling sorry for you because you're so lonely. I was afraid you'd play on his sympathy again and he'd be reluctant to break the date." She tossed her long black mane of hair again. "Don't try to make another play for him, Staci. I'm running out of patience."

"I didn't make a play for him, Marlo," I said as calmly as I could. "He asked me out and I accepted. If you're going steady with him I certainly wouldn't want to go." I felt my face flush and grow warm.

"I'm sure you wouldn't. Just remember, Staci. B.J.'s mine. If you try one of your hard luck stories on him again, one of those so-so sad little tales of woe about your mommy and all, I'll ruin you in school. I'll never give you a chance to make any friends before I let the entire student body know what a weird family you come from."

"You wouldn't dare."

"Yes I would. Wouldn't I, girls?" She turned to her friends and they smiled maliciously and nodded. "See? I would. I think the story about your mother is pretty fishy. She probably ran off with the milkman."

I felt the blood drain away from my face as I

listened to the other girls start giggling. I tried to speak, but I couldn't make any words come out.

Then, from out of nowhere, a blond streak of fury sped across the room and grabbed Marlo's perfect black mane. It was Beth.

"You don't know anything about my mother!" she yelled. "So just leave our family alone!"

By the time the librarian reached the table, Beth was gone. As quickly as she'd attacked, she disappeared, leaving a shocked Marlo gasping for breath. I realized vaguely that Beth had run outside.

"What is the meaning of this?" the librarian cried. "This is a library! Where did that little girl go?"

I turned my back on Marlo and walked away, dragging a stunned Rooster behind me. I had had all I was going to take from Marlo Cate. For all I cared she could call her rich father, the police, the whole army if she wanted. I intended to fight back in every way I could.

Rooster and I combed the library and every bush, tree, and building from there to our house—but nowhere did we find Beth. Of all us kids, Beth was the most even-tempered. She rarely lost her composure and almost never hit anyone, even Rooster, who could drive her crazy on one of his bad days.

When we reached the house the door was

still locked, and I started to get scared. Lucki-
ly, when I searched the backyard I noticed
Andy peering over the hedges.

"What happened, you guys? What's the matter?"

"Beth's gone," I said. "I don't know if she's
lost or if she ran away on purpose. We were in
the library, ran into Marlo and she said a
whole bunch of mean things. When she said
something about Mom, Beth fought back. Before I could do anything, Andy, she was gone.
Rooster and I thought she'd be outside but we
can't find her anywhere."

Andy groaned. "Leave it to Marlo to cause
something like this. Did you call your dad?"

"No! Andy, he'd have a fit if he knew about
this. Dad thinks we should never do things to
draw attention to ourselves or make people
think we're not being raised properly." I sank
into the grass. We'd tried hard, Rooster, Beth
and I, to live up to our father's expectations.
And the one thing Marlo had said that had
hurt so much was that we were inferior to B.J.
and their friends. Dad's idea might be good in
theory but it would never work in real life.
People only respected you if you respected
yourself. I'd been letting Marlo get away with
a lot of really hateful things.

Now Beth, sweet little Beth, who couldn't
stand to hear bad things about Mom, was
paying for my weakness. Mine and Dad's.

Andy was watching me. "We can't worry
right now about your dad throwing a fit, Staci.

The only thing we should consider is finding
Beth. Don't you have any idea where she
might have gone?"

"No. We looked everywhere we could think
of between here and the library. I've tried to
think where I would go if I were her but it
doesn't work." I shook my head and stared at
the ground.

"Okay," Andy said. "She's out there some-
where. All we have to do is think like she was
thinking when she ran out of the library."

"I'm not sure we can do that, Andy. She was
really upset, more furious than I thought possible."

"She pulled Marlo's hair," Rooster said, almost grinning. "She was really brave. It was
terrific!"

"I'm sure it was, Rooster," Andy said. "But
she's scared now. Afraid to come home."

"Where would you have gone if you'd got
upset at her age?" I was staring at Andy,
willing him to come up with a magic formula
for finding Beth.

He thought for a minute. Then he slapped
his palm to his forehead. "I'll bet I know
where she is, Staci. Remember how I told you
she loved the monkeys at the zoo? I'll bet
anything she's down there leaning against
those windows, crying her eyes out while she
watches the monkeys."

"Let's go! I'll leave the back door unlocked
in case she comes home."

A few minutes later we were running down the street like crazy heading for the zoo. Andy and I each had one of Rooster's hands in ours and he was practically flying through the air.

By the time the three of us reached the monkey house, my heart was pounding wildly. I tried not to think about what we'd do if Beth wasn't here. It was getting late and soon we'd have to call Dad, tell him the truth, and get help in the search.

"There she is!" Rooster screamed.

Several people turned to stare at us but I didn't care. I could see Beth leaning against the glass and watching a huge gorilla, exactly as Andy had predicted. She looked up, saw us, and started to run. Then, her small shoulders slumped and she stood still, waiting for us to catch up.

"Beth," I cried, grabbing her tightly in my arms and hugging her with all my might. "We've been scared to death. Don't worry about Marlo. You did right, you did exactly what I should have done a long time ago."

"But Dad's going to be mad," she sobbed. "And I'm probably gonna be kicked out of the library for the rest of my life."

"No you won't. If I have to, I'll tell the librarian the whole story. She'll understand."

Rooster was jumping around like one of the monkeys. "Oh, Beth," he said. "I was afraid we'd never see you again."

She smiled at us but her eyes were wet and

her lips were quivering. "Come on, honey," I said. "Let's get you home before Dad tries to reach us and finds out we're not there."

On the way home we all stopped for a snow cone at the little stand. Beth kept hiccuping every few minutes and pretty soon we were all laughing, even Beth.

"One thing I've got to say," Andy grinned. "Living next door to the Callahans is anything but dull. If you're not pounding on my window in the middle of the night, you're weathering some crisis with a sick cat or a pail of water." He laughed and ruffled Beth's blond hair. "I can't think of better neighbors."

"I can't either," I said, looking into Andy's warm green eyes. "I don't know what I'd have done without you today."

We finished our snow cones and walked on home, discussing the imminent arrival of Harvey's kittens and making wagers about how many she would have.

The phone was ringing as we walked in the back door. I hurried to answer it while Andy and the kids went in search of Harvey.

"Hello?"

"Staci, this is Stan."

"Yeah, Stan. What's up?" My heart was doing little flips again as I thought how fast Marlo must have started her rumor mill churning.

"I talked to Marlo a few minutes ago. She's really messed up with you and your family. I thought you might need a friendly ear, someone to tell you that there are several of us who have decided she's gone too far."

I held the phone away from my ear for a second, gazing at it as if there must be some mistake. "You don't believe her?" I asked finally.

"No. I guess everyone of us has been victimized by her little games at one time or another. I know Marlo is jealous because B.J. likes you. She also never wanted another girl in the astronomy club. She's run off two others that I know of."

"Thanks, Stan. It was nice of you to call. I guess I was that convinced everyone would believe Marlo and that there was no point trying to defend myself."

"Wrong. Several of us made kind of a pact this afternoon. We don't intend to speak to her until she apologizes. And those girls who are helping spread these dumb stories are going to find themselves in the same boat."

"What about B.J.?" I asked, afraid I already knew the answer.

"He's a different story. I guess B.J. Keller is one of the nicest guys I've ever met except where Marlo's concerned. Then he becomes a real jerk. I can't speak for B.J. but I'm telling you the rest of us in the club and a lot of our friends have had it with Marlo."

"Thanks," I repeated numbly. "I really appreciate this, Stan. I won't forget how nice you've been."

"Ah, we've probably been waiting for a

chance to put her in her place. Just count on us when school starts and promise me you'll come to club next week."

"I'll be there, Stan."

"Good. We'll see you then. Bye."

"Bye." I hung up the phone thinking how great these kids in Seattle were. Maybe leaving Federal Way hadn't been the end of my life after all.

Andy was standing in the doorway, grinning. "So, it sounds like old Marlo is finally getting hers."

"Yeah, I think she might be. I'm really impressed by the way that Stan Franke and his friends are sticking up for me. They don't have to do this."

Andy just grinned. "I'm glad they are, though. Makes me believe in the goodness of the human soul and all that stuff."

"It does, doesn't it?"

We watched TV for a couple of hours and then Andy went home so I could start dinner. Rooster and Beth played quietly in the den. Both of them seemed subdued and I understood perfectly. We weren't out of the woods on the Marlo thing until we got past Dad. If he found out, we were sure to catch a lot of flak. Especially if he found out Mom's name had been brought up and that was what caused most of the trouble.

Dinner was ready and the table was set when Dad came through the door. He looked at all three of us kind of funny but he didn't say anything while we ate. Not a word. Rooster and Beth picked at their food and I stopped even trying to eat.

Finally Dad pushed his plate back and looked at us. His face was hard and I could see his jaw had gotten firm and square.

"So," he said. "I got a call at work this afternoon. It seems the three of you caused a scene at the library."

"But, Dad . . ." I said.

"Don't interrupt, Staci! There are several things I'm going to discuss with you and you're going to listen. You think you can pull the wool over my eyes any time you like. The incident at the pool is another example. You may not realize this but Marlo Cate's father is a director down at my office. He made it a point to tell me today, after I'd already been humiliated by a librarian, about Rooster pushing his daughter in the pool."

He was pounding the end of his fork on the table, watching us and getting angrier by the second. "Just what kind of children am I raising? What am I supposed to do? Stay home from work every day and police you kids? Staci, you're sixteen and you've disappointed me more than I can say. I entrusted you with a responsibility and you let me down. Instead of behaving like well-brought children, the three of you have been running around Seattle wreaking havoc and getting yourselves evicted from public facilities."

"That's not the way it is, Dad. Don't you

want to hear our side of the story?" He glared at me and I closed my mouth.

"I'm not going to tolerate any more scenes. Do you understand? Beth, I expect you to call Marlo tonight and tell her you're sorry. Rooster, you're to do the same thing. Staci, I'm not sure exactly what I'm going to do about your poor performance around here this summer. For starters, consider yourself grounded until further notice."

I was stunned. I'd expected Dad to be angry if he found out but I'd never dreamed he wouldn't listen to our side. Beth was looking at Dad and her small pretty features looked like a duplicate of Mom's when she'd been angry. It was almost like Mom was back, sitting there at the table with us. "I'm not going to do it, Daddy," Beth said. "I don't care if you ground me until I'm a hundred. I won't call Marlo and tell her I'm sorry. Because I'm not sorry. Not one bit." Beth stood up and shoved her plate back. "Marlo said Mom wasn't dead. She told all those girls that Mama ran off with a milkman!"

The color drained from my father's face. It was just like they're always saying in books but I didn't think it was possible until that moment. His hand went up to his chest and for a horrible moment I thought he might have a heart attack. He looked at me, his eyes bulging with disbelief. "Is this true, Staci? Did she actually say that?"

I nodded.

Rooster stood up and pushed his plate back, too, emulating his sister. "I won't say I'm sorry, either! She said you were making Staci raise us because Mama was too lazy to do it herself. That's why I pushed her in the pool." Rooster was just about to cry but his eyes were flashing like Beth's and I could tell he wasn't going to back down.

It was my turn. I followed the kids' example, standing up and shoving my plate away. "Dad, I don't care how long you ground me. Rooster and Beth did right to defend Mom."

Daddy stood up, too. The four of us stood around the table like we were having some sort of showdown. Rooster and Beth moved over beside me and I got ready for Dad to really let us have it. But he just looked at us and then he sank back into his chair and buried his forehead in his hands. His shoulders were shaking and I knew he was crying. I didn't know what to do.

Finally Dad looked up. "Why didn't you tell me things like this were going on?"

"We couldn't tell you, Dad," I gasped, truthfully surprised. "You won't even let us talk about the good times with Mom, won't even mention her name. I figured if you knew about this you'd really get mad."

"Why can't we talk about Mama?" Rooster was looking at Dad, begging for an answer.

He groaned and I could still see tears in his

eyes. "It's too painful," he said. "I thought the less we talked about her the easier it would be for us to go on, try to make a life without her."

"But we loved her, Dad," I cried. "Not being able to talk about her makes the empty place in our life bigger, seems to almost scream at us that she's gone. You've even hidden her pictures away where we can't find them. Sometimes I can't picture her face anymore and I get scared." I was crying. So were Rooster and Beth.

Dad held out his arms and we ran to him, tumbling into a hug I'd been afraid we'd never feel again. "Come on," he said in a husky voice. "Let's go get those pictures. Then I think it's time for this family to have a long talk."

10

We talked until after midnight, looking at pictures of Mom and saying all those things we'd kept hidden inside for two years. Rooster and Beth seemed to blossom before my eyes when Dad hung a large portrait of Mom over the fireplace.

There was a lot of crying and hugging and I went to bed feeling as if our family had been re-born. I knew there would still be rough times when my father and I would disagree or the kids would fuss over silly things like which TV show to watch or who got to sit by the window in the front seat of the car. But stuff like that would happen even if Mom were here. The important thing was that we could talk now, remember freely the mother who'd loved us all so much.

The sun seemed brighter than usual when I woke Thursday morning. Brilliant shadows danced on my bedroom walls and the whole room felt cozy, like it finally belonged to me as surely as my room in Federal Way had. I jumped out of bed without grumbling or even rolling over wishing for a few more minutes of sleep. I could hear the shower running and knew Dad was already up, so I dressed and hurried down to make his breakfast.

He was in a good mood. I heard him singing "Sweet Rosie O'Grady" as he came down the stairs, a song he'd often sung back in Federal Way. When he came into the kitchen he gave me a big hug before he sat down at the table and opened the paper.

"It feels good, being a family again. Doesn't it?" I asked, handing him a plate of scrambled eggs and bacon.

"It certainly does, Staci. Your mother would be proud of us if she were here. She would have wanted us to be strong." He looked down at his plate for a moment. "Remember what big dreams she had for you? What high hopes she had for all three of her children?"

I smiled. My mother had believed we could do anything we set our minds to do. I knew it was her influence that had given me the faith to dare to dream of becoming an astronaut. "I remember," I said. "She was pretty special."

"Very. And from now on we'll never let ourselves hide those memories away. I put something in your room this morning, Staci.

Your mother kept a journal; she wrote in it nearly every night after she found out she was going to have you." He drained his coffee cup, looking thoughtful. "I almost threw that book away after she died. In nearly every entry you'll find evidence of the unique way your mother had of looking at life."

I hugged Dad, feeling as if I might cry again. His gift was one of the most touching things he'd ever done for me. I knew it couldn't have been easy for him to part with Mom's journal. I'd seen it lying beside her bed for years, but I'd never read it, not a word. It was such a private thing, such a special part of my mother, that I knew I'd treasure it forever. I couldn't wait until things got quiet tonight so I could curl up with that book and get lost in memories of Mom.

My father gave me another hug and left for work. I hurried to clean the kitchen and get ready for Rooster and Beth who would be charging downstairs at any time. This morning I planned to feed them cold cereal so I could work on my telescope and maybe have time to sit around and talk with Andy this afternoon. He'd be very pleased with the way things were turning out for the Callahans.

I owed Andy Warren a lot and my thoughts of him were warm and friendly this morning. In fact, it surprised me just how much I was thinking about him. I kept seeing his green eyes in my mind and remembering the good advice he'd given me about Dad, and my

obligation to make him talk to us about Mom.
If it hadn't have been for Andy, I realized,
Rooster, Beth, and I might still be sitting
around feeling sorry for ourselves over the
library incident and stinging from making
apologies to Marlo Cate that were totally un-
warranted.

I'd just finished straightening the kitchen
and putting bowls and juice glasses out for the
kids when they came tearing into the kitchen.

"Harvey's sick," Rooster cried. "Really sick
this time, Staci. We can't get her to stand up
or anything."

"Where is she?" I asked.

"On my bed," Beth said. Her eyes were big
and round and her voice caught in her throat,
making a weird croaking sound.

"Okay, let's go have a look at her," I said,
feeling my good emotions give way to fear.
Rooster and Beth seemed awfully scared and
I felt certain Harvey was worse than she'd
been the other times.

"Maybe she's having the kittens," I told
them, trying to sound more cheerful than I
felt. "It's surely time."

We all ran up to Beth's room where I found
Harvey lying on the bed. Her eyes were glazed
and I could tell that she was in pain. The kids
piled onto the bed beside her and she let out a
pitiful meow.

My stomach twisted with fear. I knew nothing about kittens being born but I didn't think

it should be like this. "Do you know how long she's been doing this, Beth?"

Beth shook her head.

"All right. I want you two to run over and get Andy. I'll put Harvey on a blanket and take her down to the den. Hurry. Just tell him I'm pretty sure she's having her kittens."

They ran out of the room and I got an old quilt from the linen closet, moved Harvey onto it gently and carried her downstairs. I placed the quilt on the floor and stroked Harvey's head, waiting for Andy and the kids. Soon they were back, tearing into the room and crowding close.

"Get back," I told the kids. "Let Andy look at her."

"But I saw a film at school," Beth said. "I know a lot about baby kittens." She was hovering in Harvey's face, looking in the poor cat's mouth.

"What are you doing?" I yelled.

"Looking for babies."

"They won't come out of her mouth. Now get back. You're scaring her to death."

Beth was sulking as she pulled away. "They came out of that other cat's mouth. In the film I saw."

"Must have been some film." Andy grinned, gently moving both kids away from Harvey. He stroked her and talked to her softly, examining her as he talked. "I think there's a problem, Staci. It looks like there are two kittens coming at once." He straightened up and turned to me. "Will you call a vet and see if we can get her in right away?"

"Where are two kittens?" Rooster cried. "I want to see.."

"Not now, Rooster. Harvey's not feeling very well. If you want to help her, the best thing you can do is stay back. When the kittens are born you can have a look."

I thumbed through the phone book. "What was that doctor's name? The one down by the Safeway?"

"Dr. Stanton. Fred, I think."

I dialed the number, explained the problem and then waited while the girl who'd answered the phone went to talk to the doctor. She came back on the line. "Can you bring your cat down to the office right away? Dr. Stanton thinks he should see her."

"I'll be there as soon as I can," I said, hanging the phone up and turning to Andy. "He wants to see her. Could you drive me down there?"

"Sure." He kept smiling and trying to act cheerful even though I could tell he was worried. "I think I'll take these two monkeys over to stay with Mom." He put a hand on each of the kids' shoulders and gazed at me over their heads. "I'd rather they not go along."

I nodded, feeling the knot of fear in my stomach grow tighter. "Do you think she'll mind?"

"Not at all. She's been waiting all summer for a chance to watch these kids."

"I'm not going," Beth said, seating herself close to Harvey and folding her arms over her chest in that determined pose she adopted when she'd made up her mind about something.

"I want to stay with Harvey," Rooster said. His blue eyes looked almost wild and his bottom lip was quivering.

"You guys are going to have to trust me," Andy said. "Harvey needs help and there's nothing you can do for her right now. As soon as Staci and I know something we'll call you." He smiled at them and ruffled their hair. "Dr. Stanton is good. He's the one who sewed up Bozo's leg after he got caught in that fence."

Rooster smiled a little. "Bozo's okay. He runs just as well as ever now."

"That's right. If the doctor could help Bozo that much he can help Harvey, too. So, come on. I'll take you to my house and you can help Mom eat the mountain of cookies she was baking this morning."

They both gave Harvey one last look and followed Andy to the back door. "I'll come to the front with the car," he said. "Do you think you can carry her out there on that quilt?"

"Sure." My fists were clenching and unclenching. "Please hurry, Andy."

He was back in a few minutes, pulling up in front of the house in his old Volkswagen. He had a large cardboard box on the back seat, and we carefully put Harvey, quilt and all, in the box. I climbed into the front seat.

"Do you think she's going to be all right, Andy?"

For the first time he let his real concern show. "I don't know. Dr. Stanton can do a lot for her, I'm sure. But I don't see how he can save those kittens. There are at least two of them trying to be born at the same time."

Andy didn't speed but he drove as fast as possible, skillfully maneuvering the Volkswagen through traffic. It took only about five minutes to reach Dr. Stanton's office but it seemed much longer than that to me. Andy and I carried the box inside together. I watched Harvey, noticing how exhausted she looked. She made no attempt to move as we carried her across the parking lot.

The receptionist ushered us into an examining room right away. Everything smelled clinical and antiseptic. My fear grew as we waited for the doctor. Once Andy squeezed my hand but mostly we just watched Harvey, stroking her every so often to let her know we were there.

The door opened and Dr. Stanton walked in. He was a huge man with a warm smile. "Let me have a look at your little mother," he said, leaning over the box. "I think we'd better take her out of there." Soon, with Andy's help, the doctor had Harvey lying on her quilt on the steel table.

After examining her, he turned to me. "I'm going to have to do a cesarean section, young lady. Those babies are wedged pretty tight. And I'm afraid this mama is just too tired to help herself anymore. Have you any idea how long she's been trying to have these kittens?"

I shook my head, feeling guilty, as if I should know a thing like that. "She was like this when my sister woke up this morning. Harvey was at the foot of the bed, just lying there the way she is now."

"Harvey?" He smiled at the cat. "I guess you're in for an experience as unusual as your name. I don't have to do this very often."

"What about the kittens?" I asked, hearing the quiver in my voice and dreading the answer to my question.

Dr. Stanton shook his head slowly. "I can't answer that. A lot depends on how long she's been trying to have them." He reached out, patted my shoulder and smiled. "I do know this. They're alive right now. I want you to go home and wait for me to call. The operation should take about an hour. Give your phone number to my receptionist and I'll call you the minute I'm through."

I had no choice and after giving Harvey one last pat on the head, I followed Andy out of the examining room. We gave the girl at the desk my number and walked slowly to Andy's car.

"I'm scared, Andy," I said as he drove home. My eyes were spilling tears onto my cheeks faster than I could wipe them away.

"Harvey looks so tired. As though she might just stop breathing because it's too much work."

"I know she looks bad. But if anyone can help her, I think Dr. Stanton can." He squeezed my hand. "What are we going to tell Rooster and Beth? You know they'll come running over the minute they see the car."

"I'm going to tell them the truth, Andy. If we let them get their hopes up and then something happens, they'll never trust me again." I sighed and felt tears close. "They're so little, Andy. Just how much should they have to take?"

"I don't know, Staci. But can't you have a little faith? You don't know things won't turn out all right. Maybe Harvey and the kittens will all be fine."

We had reached my house. Andy pulled into the driveway and jumped out of the car. I saw Rooster and Beth running across the lawn and groaned. I'd told Andy I wasn't going to lie to the kids but the idea of explaining everything seemed like too much to bear right then.

"Where's Harvey?" Rooster cried. "Where are the babies?"

Both kids were bobbing up and down like yo-yos. Their expressions were a confusion of hope and fear. Somehow I suddenly lost all my nerve. I didn't have the heart to tell them everything, take away that shred of hope that burned in their eyes.

Andy looked at me. "She had to stay with

Dr. Stanton for a while. He's taking care of her and the babies and he'll call us when it's time to come back and get them."

I glared at Andy, wondering if he intended to hang around and tell Rooster and Beth what had happened if something went wrong. Now there was no way I could tell the kids what was going on, even if I had the nerve. They had bought Andy's story, hook, line, and sinker. Hope and belief had wiped the fear from their faces. I moved toward the house slowly, dreading the doctor's phone call but afraid to miss it.

I stomped into the den to wait for the phone call.

Andy followed me. "If you think you can stop dwelling on your morbid thoughts, would you like to play Monopoly?"

"Sure. Why not. Maybe we can send up a couple of flares later and shoot off some fireworks."

He pulled the game off the shelf beside the couch, ignoring my sarcasm. "Rooster and Beth went upstairs to make a bed for Harvey and the kittens. Do you think you could restrain yourself from getting a shovel and digging Harvey's grave until you hear from Dr. Stanton?"

"Very funny, Andy. Just because I'm a realist, you think it's your moral obligation to change me, make me believe in fairy tales and happy endings because you do."

He grinned, infuriating me even more. "It's

not a bad way to live, Staci. Every once in a while life does hand you a happy ending. I prefer to expect them."

I was tapping my foot nervously against the couch. "Are we going to play this dumb game or sit around and discuss the deeper philosophies of one Andy Warren?"

"Both." He laughed and counted out the Monopoly money.

"Why doesn't the doctor call?" I asked, tapping the couch with more force.

"He said it would be at least an hour," Andy replied patiently.

"How long has it been?"

"Twenty or thirty minutes. It's your turn."

I shook the dice and landed on Oriental. "I'll buy it," I said.

Before long I owned all the blue, orange, and yellow properties.

"You're lucky when you're worried," Andy said, grinning good-naturedly. "The only thing I'm gonna end up with are the railroads."

"Why doesn't that doctor call?" I said, jumping up and pacing around the room. "And don't tell me it hasn't been an hour. We've been here longer than that."

"Relax, Staci. He's a good doctor and I'm sure he's doing everything he can. Maybe there are things he hadn't counted on."

The phone rang and I lunged across the den to answer it.

"Hello?"

"Staci, this is Dr. Stanton."

"How's Harvey?" I cried. "Is she all right?"

"Well, are you ready to come get six squalling babies and one sleepy mama?"

"Yes. Oh, yes. We'll be right there." I hung up the phone and turned to see Andy looking at me. He was smiling and I could have sworn I saw a tear in his eye.

"Happy ending?" he asked.

I nodded. "Sounds like it. Andy, I'm sorry I was so cross."

"No sweat." He went to the bottom of the stairs. "Hey, kids. Get down here."

They came tearing down the stairs, their faces searching mine and Andy's for some clue about Harvey.

"Things are pretty good," Andy said. "Now, if you two will go over to my house, we'll go get your cat."

"How many babies, Staci? How many?" Rooster was clutching at me and he looked happy enough to burst.

I smiled at him. "Six, Rooster. I think that means I won the bet."

Beth kept grinning but she was crying at the same time. "The bed's all ready for them," she said proudly. "It's really pretty. I bet Harvey will love it."

"I'm sure she will, honey. Now both of you run over and stay with Mrs. Warren. We'll be back as soon as we can."

Andy and I were excited as we drove to the

doctor's office. As soon as we arrived we were ushered into the examining room again. Harvey was sound asleep. The tiny kittens were lying in the box beside her.

"Are they all right?" I managed to ask.

"Well," Dr. Stanton said, "they need their mother's warmth and I doubt if she'll be able to take them for several hours. I don't think you'll save them all but you should save the strongest ones."

I leaned over the box. "Is Harvey all right?"

"Oh, she's fine," Dr. Stanton said. "Once the anesthetic wears off she'll look much better. She's going to be sore for a while but I think you'll be surprised how fast she recovers. I want you to get these kittens home and try to keep them warm with a heating pad or a light bulb. Put a little syrup in their mouths with an eye-dropper every hour or so. You should be able to save the strongest ones if you work at it."

I almost stumbled as we walked to the desk where I gave the doctor our address and some information about Dad's office so he could send a bill. Andy was carrying the box.

"By the way," Dr. Stanton said. "Be sure to put the mother in another box when you get home. I don't want those kittens going to her until she's fully awake and that could be several hours." He smiled. "Good luck, Staci."

"Thanks," I said. "Thanks for all your help."

Andy and I were silent as we put the box in the car. Finally, when he was backing the car and turning around, Andy spoke. "I'm sorry, Staci. But if we try really hard maybe we can save at least one kitten for each of the kids."

I looked at him fiercely. "I'm going to save every one of these kittens! Rooster and Beth aren't going to have to see even one of them die."

"But you heard the doctor. He said you'd only save the strongest ones."

I looked at him and watched his beautiful green eyes flash. "So, I changed my mind. I've got a chance to save them and I'm going to do it."

"Women sure start being women awfully young," Andy muttered as he turned into my driveway.

The kids reached the house almost as quickly as Andy and I. They were pulling and hauling on the box until Andy told them to stand back and let us get inside. As soon as we were in the house, he sat the box down and let them look. For some dumb reason the kids thought those scrawny, wet kittens were beautiful.

"Okay," I said. "All of you get away. I have a lot to do to keep these babies warm. Andy, will you take Harvey up to her bed and help Rooster and Beth keep an eye on her?"

He nodded. As he reached into the box for Harvey he smiled. "You don't have to do this alone, Staci. There are other hands willing to help. Do you think you're the only one who can save these kittens?"

"I said I'd do it and I will. Now if you'd please get the kids out of here I'd appreciate it."

"Your servant," he said, bowing from the waist before he lifted Harvey gently in his arms and started up the stairs.

I carried the box of kittens to the kitchen and closed the door behind me. The heating pad was in the cupboard over the dryer and I pulled it down, plugged it in and set the dial on warm. Then I covered the kittens with a light towel and scurried around fixing a bowl of syrup and finding an old eye-dropper. While I waited to see how the heating pad was going to work, I brought a lamp in from Dad's desk and removed the shade, getting it ready in case the first method didn't work.

Ten minutes later I peeked at the kittens and was horrified to find they hadn't dried much and they still seemed cold. I was just getting ready to warm them with the lamp in addition to using the heating pad when there was a knock on the back door.

I opened it to find Andy's mother standing on the porch with a plate of cookies in her hand. I hadn't seen her since the day I'd thrown my crying fit and I looked down, a little ashamed and also a bit impatient at the interruption.

Mrs. Warren put out her arms and gave me a big hug, almost spilling the cookies all over the floor. "How are you doing, honey?" she asked. "Andy tells me you're having a pretty exciting day." Before I could answer she was walking across the kitchen and lifting the towel off the kittens. "Well, aren't they cute? Is the mother all right?"

I nodded. "She's upstairs. The anesthetic hasn't worn off yet. Mrs. Warren, could you please cover the kittens again? The doctor said if I didn't keep them warm some of them would die."

"Oh, my dear, I'm sorry. Can I help?"

"I can't get them warm enough, or dry," I said. "I'm scared they're all going to die and Rooster and Beth will blame me."

She hugged me. Didn't ask a bunch of stupid questions or tell me I'd been a jerk, she just hugged me. The kitchen door opened and there was Rooster.

"Andy told us how the kittens need Harvey to be warm," he said. "If they need her body and she's asleep, wouldn't our bodies work?"

I stared at him and then at the box of cold, wet kittens. Now Rooster stood before me with the perfect answer. Of course it would work. I wondered why the vet hadn't thought of it himself. "Yes, Rooster," I cried. "Your body will work! And so will mine and Beth's and Andy's. You're a very smart little boy and I love you very much." I was almost dancing around the kitchen and Andy's mother was watching me with a great big Andyish smile on her face.

"I'm going to go fix a dinner large enough for both families," she said. "You kids keep up your good work and I'll see you later." With another hug around my neck, she was gone.

Rooster was still standing there. "Go get everyone, silly," I cried. "We've got a litter of kittens to save."

He ran out of the room, laughing that special Rooster laugh of his that telegraphed his delight in himself all through the house.

The four of us sat down on the kitchen floor and looked at our pitiful little charges. Then I slipped one inside Rooster's shirt and another in Beth's. "Rub them carefully," I instructed. "Keep them against your skin and stroke them as softly as possible until they're dry and warm."

I handed two kittens to Andy and took two myself. The kitchen was quiet as we held and warmed the babies. A couple of times I glanced at Andy and he was watching me with a look that said I'd done something right for a change. And I felt I had. When I'd first slipped my kittens inside my shirt I had felt how chilled and sluggish they were. But now, over an hour later, I could feel warm, wiggling life squirming around and nuzzling my skin. "Let's take them out now," I whispered. "They need a drop of syrup."

There was a hushed silence as Rooster and Beth slowly pulled fluffy kittens out of soft warm shirts. Andy and I did the same. The babies looked healthy now. And full of life.

They took the syrup in their mouths almost greedily and then we slid them back against our skin, warming them the best way we knew how.

When Dad came in I explained the whole story and, after taking a look at the kittens and grumbling good-naturedly about the doctor's bill, he went over to Andy's house for supper. We held the kittens for hours, feeding them syrup every so often and petting their tiny bodies gently.

Dad brought food back for all of us and we ate, careful not to disturb the kittens even though I felt certain they'd be all right if we put them on the heating pad for awhile. The hours with the kittens were special, something I wouldn't have traded for anything. My father even went up and got Harvey, bringing her down and setting her box in a dark corner of the kitchen so we'd know when she woke up.

I'd worried a little that she was sleeping too long. But she looked better than she had when we picked her up from Dr. Stanton.

At ten o'clock, Dad made Rooster and Beth go to bed. They gave their small charges to Andy and me and we sat far into the night, holding three squirming kittens each. A few times we talked, but mostly we just sat there and enjoyed the quiet time.

Once I looked over at Andy and wondered how I'd have made it through the day without him. And my mind re-created a dozen memories of times when he'd been there to help me and be my friend when things went wrong in my life. "Thanks, Andy," I whispered. "I guess you're about the best friend a person could have."

I looked at him, really looked. He was the warmest, sweetest person I had ever known and I felt like a fool for not noticing it before. I looked into those fabulous green eyes and felt something weird in my stomach. It was maybe the best feeling I'd ever had, certainly better than the feeling when I'd kissed B.J. Keller.

Just then Harvey woke up and meowed. Not a painful sound, more like a "where are my babies" sound. Andy and I hurried over, saw she was fully awake, and then we carried the kittens to her, placing them gently in the box. She began to purr and lick their faces.

"Go get the kids, Andy. Will you? They've earned the right to see this."

He grinned and nodded.

Soon Rooster and Beth were standing sleepily beside the box, oohing and aahing over Harvey and the kittens.

"There's mine," Rooster said, rubbing his eyes. "I'm going to keep it forever and ever."

"Me, too," Beth said. She looked angelic in the dim light.

And suddenly Mom's face was there in my mind, laughing in that special way she had that always made me want to crawl up on her lap and give her the world's biggest hug, even when I got older. Her face was in front of me and, in my mind, I could see she would have been pleased with the way things had turned out today, maybe pleased with the way Rooster, Beth, and I were turning out. The picture was so clear I almost felt I could touch her if I tried. She smiled at me, there in my mind, and then she was gone, leaving the warmest feeling I'd ever known. And I knew she'd be back, knew I'd be able to picture her whenever I wanted to from now on.

I walked Andy to the back door after the kids went back to bed. "Good-night, friend," I said. "You're terrific."

Our eyes met again but this time there was no cat to interrupt us and no kids tearing through the room. I looked at Andy and he looked at me. A long gaze that said so much about the twelve years of friendship between the two of us.

And then Andy Warren kissed me. My heart was beating in my ears and there was a wonderful song playing in my head. I kissed Andy back, marveling at how much more exciting this kiss was than the one I'd shared with B.J. This kiss felt good all over, from head to toe. There was a feeling of "rightness" about kissing Andy.

He hugged me and I put my arms around him, feeling the warmth of his chest, a warmth that had helped give life to kittens just hours before. I wanted to keep kissing Andy but I knew we'd stop. We were like that.

He smiled at me, kissed my forehead, and went out the door.

I watched him run across the yard and jump the hedge, catching his shoe on the top and falling noisily to the other side. My heart felt it might explode with feelings for Andy.

I walked over and watched Harvey feed her kittens in the dimly lit kitchen. I remembered Rooster and his brilliant idea for saving the babies. Suddenly, everything seemed clear. People, like kittens, needed body warmth to survive. Dad, Rooster, Beth and I had almost learned that fact last night. But it had taken a little boy's love for a cat to complete the lesson.

As for Andy, I think he'd always known.

Three exciting *First Love from Silhouette romances* yours for 15 days—*free!*

If you enjoyed this First Love from Silhouette® you'll want to read more! These are true-to-life romances about the things that matter most to you now—your friendships, dating, getting along in school, and learning about yourself. The stories could really happen, and the characters are so real they'll seem like friends.

Now you can get 3 First Love from Silhouette romances to look over for 15 days—absolutely free! If you decide not to keep them, simply return them and pay nothing. But if you enjoy them as much as we believe you will, keep them and pay the invoice enclosed with your trial shipment. You'll then become a member of the First Love from Silhouette℠ Book Club and will receive 3 more new First Love from Silhouette romances every month. You'll always be among the first to get them, and you'll never miss a new title. There is no minimum number of books to buy and you can cancel at any time. To receive your 3 books, mail the coupon below today.

First Love from Silhouette® is a service mark and a registered trademark of Simon & Schuster.

First Love from Silhouette

THERE'S NOTHING QUITE AS SPECIAL AS A FIRST LOVE.

$1.75 each

1 ☐ NEW BOY IN TOWN
Francis

2 ☐ GIRL IN THE ROUGH
Wunsch

3 ☐ PLEASE LET ME IN
Beckman

4 ☐ SERENADE
Marceau

5 ☐ FLOWERS FOR LISA
Ladd

6 ☐ KATE HERSELF
Erskine

7 ☐ SONGBIRD
Enfield

10 ☐ PLEASE LOVE ME . . .
SOMEBODY Johnson

11 ☐ IT'S MY TURN
Carr

12 ☐ IN MY SISTER'S SHADOW
Dellin

13 ☐ SOMETIME MY LOVE
Ryan

14 ☐ PROMISED KISS
Ladd

15 ☐ SUMMER ROMANCE
Diamond

16 ☐ SOMEONE TO LOVE
Bryan

17 ☐ GOLDEN GIRL
Erskine

18 ☐ WE BELONG TOGETHER
Harper

19 ☐ TOMORROW'S WISH
Ryan

20 ☐ SAY PLEASE!
Francis

21 ☐ TEACH ME TO LOVE
Davis

22 ☐ THAT SPECIAL SUMMER
Kent

$1.95 each

23 ☐ WHEN SEPTEMBER
RETURNS Jones

24 ☐ DREAM LOVER
Treadwell

25 ☐ THE PERSONAL TOUCH
Cooney

26 ☐ A TIME FOR US
Ryan

27 ☐ A SECRET PLACE
Francis

28 ☐ LESSON IN LOVE
West

29 ☐ FOR THE LOVE OF LORI
Ladd

30 ☐ A BOY TO DREAM ABOUT
Quinn

31 ☐ THE FIRST ACT
London

32 ☐ DARE TO LOVE
Bush

33 ☐ YOU AND ME
Johnson

34 ☐ THE PERFECT FIGURE
March

First Love from Silhouette

Look for These New First Love Romances from Silhouette Books Next Month

Just Friends

Dorothy Francis

The ultimate romance . . . moonlight and roses . . . a boyfriend who would always remember her birthday, ask her to all the big events . . . that's what Jacey had always wanted. Had she chosen the wrong guy? Or was this a different kind of love?

Promises To Come

Genell Dellin

What do you do when you fall for a boy and your brothers call you "Red" and make you sound immature and boyish? Should you give up playing shortstop? Go wild with makeup? Flirt outrageously? Only Tiffany knows for sure!

A Knight To Remember

Pam Martin

Tina was sure that proud Michael Donovan, the handsome horse trainer, was unimportant in her life. First came Stan, her steady boyfriend, and then, Bell her horse. Why then, did he continue riding through her dreams?